Against her will, Madi had been brought to The Mansion.

It had been a prison once. Now it was something else. But nothing could still the silent screams of those who had never left there—alive.

Madi did not fear the evil of the past. There was a new madness that hid in the shadows of the present, a madness she had to seek out and destroy—or else stay locked in that dark world forever.

Fawcett Gold Medal Books
by Wilma Forrest:

ANNE OF DESTINY HOUSE
LAST HOPE HOUSE
SHADOW MANSION

SHADOW MANSION

by WILMA FORREST

A FAWCETT GOLD MEDAL BOOK
Fawcett Publications, Inc., Greenwich, Conn.

SHADOW MANSION

◄(CHAPTER I)►

MADI LOOKED DOWN AS SILENTLY AS the coachman did at the mansion she was to join. The coachman had a drooping sadness about him. October afternoon was gilding the impassive outer walls of the compound. A wind swept the yard and raised dust. There was a sun-glisten on shards of glass or metal that topped the walls, which must have been fifteen feet high. She could tell that the surrounding walls and the massive inner building must have been built from native stone. Stone such as this was mountain stone. Barred windows had faint light in the recesses, as if white hands were gripping them and unseen eyes were looking out. Three of the score of scattered chimneys had smoke arising from them. On all four sides of the enclosure the land had been cut over, and now grass and clover were deep for at least two hundred yards. Looking into the grass, she saw the bobbing of the cottontail of a rabbit. A hush was over the land and leaves turning made a swirl of light, like some jack-o-lanterns she had once seen.

There was some foam on the backs of the horses, and a prickling of the wind lifted flakes of it like spindrift. She smelled tobacco and turned and saw that the coachman had lighted a short, curved pipe, its bowl seared black on one side. Pipes. She remembered laughing once when bubbles had soared into the air and someone had exclaimed of castles. This was her castle below?

She thought she must have been deceived in New York at the jail. She didn't know anything much about the prison system, but she had heard some things at the jail. Prisons often were places where people who were active and strong enough worked so that a profit could be made. Maybe it was possible for a prison in one state—this one, Massachusetts—to recruit workers from jails in other states. Maybe they had tricked her into coming here on her own in order to save the money it would have cost to have her escorted?

That didn't make much sense, she thought, but what did?

She remembered the kneading room, as it was called by the veteran inmates of the jail. In the kneading room you knelt on the stone floor in front of a committee of religious people, men and women, sitting on wooden chairs, with some jail wardens standing balefully behind them. If you were a prostitute, she had heard, they offered to find you a job as a maid in a nice home if you would be willing to have your sex opening sewn. They offered to obtain for you a solitary confinement cell if you felt that the decency would give you time and privacy in which to repent.

In her own case, she had been taken to the kneading room by a burly guard who held her by the back of her dress just above her buttocks. Strangely enough her poverty had been so great that she hadn't minded his hand rubbing against her buttocks so much when he stumbled as she had minded the ripping of her garment. The offense of his hand would be in her own mind, but the ripped garment would be in the minds of all who saw her. Her last dress was the only dignity left to her in front of a world of people clothed in garments of dress, mind, and privacy that she did not possess. They should give you something to wear in jail. It was surprising how far your head would bend when your clothing was no longer dainty. She had always hated the raw smell of whiskey on a man but she did not mind it on the stumbling guard. The only thing important in the world was her dress. Not even the memory of her mother's corpse was important, gray, oddly faceless, as if her mother in jail-death had not wanted to look like herself, as if she had wanted to be effaced so that even her own daughter would not know who she was. They had let Madi look at her mother in the gray coffin with the number on it. Madi had heard that they took the coffins out to sea on barges. Perhaps her mother had been glad that a number was on the coffin and not her name. Even the fish would not have known that Mrs. Brooks went by.

"Kneel down," the guard had said. She went down stiffly. Her legs were old today. Yesterday she had worked very hard on the treadmill. It was geared in such a way that it could be worked properly by twenty women if all the women were of average strength. But one woman had been old, with her efforts showing ropes of veins in a rent in her dress. One pallid child had been vomiting. One woman was pregnant. A woman was drunk. Madi had worked very hard to make the mill work. They all had to eat, and if the mill did not make a certain number of revolutions in the eight hours, then there would be no meal.

Madi's mother had not walked the treadmill. When they had accepted father's debts (all he could belatedly think of when he was dying), Mother had been working at an upright stitching machine in a loft, and Madi has been teaching school. Blades of the stitching machine had snapped and whipped across Mother's thighs. Madi had taken care of her, there was no other way, and Madi had lost her job. The marshals had escorted them to the yellow brick fortress of a workhouse. There was no sentence, of course, it was only a jail. You stayed there until you were tried, or you stayed there until you paid your debts. Madi and her mother did not know anyone else very well. No one to ask for money.

Mother's legs could not work the treadmill, so Mother had earned her bread with the hand mill. Five pounds pressure was the rule for women, ten for men. Mother's hands were lumped from work. It was hard for her to make the ten thousand revolutions of the hand mill that were required in a day. Madi tried to give her own bread and gruel to her mother, but the answer was a shaking of the head. And the gnarled hands that had held books went slowly, painfully on and on, until late at night the task had ten thousand times been done. Two years had been ground into the mill.

Madi had knelt before five chairs that were placed in a slight semicircle. On the floor she was facing two spare clergymen to the left, and to the right one thin lady and two fat ones. The fat lady in the center had a broad grin and lips that looked as though they were suckling on an eternal sweet. She was the one that spoke.

"You are a girl of the jail," she said, nodding brightly. "Oh, my. Have you preserved yourself?"

She kept smiling, but the others glared down at Madi with immense reservation.

"Speak, girl," said the smiling woman, fanning her breast. "Have you submitted to lust?"

A blinding pain of rage and humiliation shot through Madi. She wanted to leap up and yell that her mother had been a frugal, decent person and had died because of the debts of a dissolute husband, and she wanted to scratch and yell that she too had taken her father's debts, and she wanted to rant, scream, and fight! But she knew that if she had done all this, her end would have been ignominious. She would have found her face flat on the brick floor and hard-

9

guard-breathing on her neck, and she would have been taken away by the hands and feet over the slippery rough floor (she had seen it done) and put in what was called the dispensary, where you were degraded by being stripped and used by medical students.

She thought of smashing her head against the floor, and in reaction to that very real wish she bent her head, but she did not smash it. The flame in her heart would not give them that carnival.

So they thought she bowed to them, and she heard them chuckle with satisfaction. No more answer was required of her. She had symbolically kissed clerical and welfare feet.

"We think we have a position for you, my child," said the fat, bubbling woman. "For reasons of your fairly educated background and your present consequence, it is hard to imagine someone who would be more qualified."

"Go, then, with Jesus Christ," said a male voice.

"I never had any sympathy for the South," said the coachman, "but they wasn't nice to the boys down there in that prison. My own boy was in Libbey, yep, he was there. Tried to dig out. Was one of them that tried it. A heap of it in my boy. But, miss, they wasn't any worse in Libbey or Andersonville than they was in what you're looking at."

"What is it now?" she asked.

She could feel him turn and stare at her. She turned her head and met his hound face and dog eyes. "Why, miss," he said, "that's where you're going."

"But what is it?"

"You don't know what it is?"

"I was . . . I was engaged here to take care of children. I didn't know I was being summoned to a prison."

"That ain't no prison, miss. That's a mansion. It used to be a prison. The only reason I sat here and looked at it is that my boy was in a war prison and he didn't come out so good. Whenever I see this place, I have to stop and think about that. That's all. Stop and think about it. About the way they was on both sides. I don't take sides no more. No use doin' that. It don't do no good. Plenty of heartbreak, both sides. Folks down South must think the same as us. That's no prison, miss. Folks there are as nice as you please. Colonel likes this part of the country. He was commandant there, God forgive him. But what could he do, any of us? And you can't get a building like that very easy. See how it's built? That's built for centuries. Ever heard that expression? Why, they'll fix this

10

up like a park. And it is. Just look around." He pointed his pipe at October, mountain, and prison.

"The screamin' and moanin' down there is over, miss. We had the worse war that could ever happen in creation. Brother against brother. You couldn't have anything worse than that. I'll take you down there, miss. Everything's going to be all right in this world. Nothing could ever happen that was worse than brother against brother."

In front of the prison mansion gate there was a jolly, round woman sitting on a chair and shelling peas into her open lap. Her face was as round as her belly. Her smile took over her entire face. She stood up, holding the apron, and deftly poured the peas into a pail. "Hello, John," she said to the coachman.

"Makin' dinner?" he asked.

"Yay-es, John. Stay if you want. Now, that's a likely young lady you have up there."

"Brought her all the way by hand. This coach always has pretty young ladies."

"First time I ever knew it," she said. "Miss Brooks?"

"Yes, ma'am."

"I've been waiting here for two hours. Always knew this coach couldn't get anywhere on time. Where's the mail, John?"

"Ain't none this time."

"Hand the young lady down, or do you want me to do your work for you?"

"Work? You? Sittin' out in the sun all the time making a mess of peas?"

"You won't mind the soup if you come back tomorrow with some mail."

"Who's writin' to you?"

"I never got a letter in my life, but I'm always hoping."

"I'll send you one."

"You can't write, you old crock."

"I can prove you're wrong."

"You got this girl's trunk?"

"I'm gettin' old, you lift it."

The coachman handed Madi down to the plump woman, and the woman said, "I'm Elvira Pancoast. Charge of the house. Been that for years." Her hands were dimpled and warm on Madi's. "Live around here. All my life. This mansion has been a good part of it. My husband and me. It's a caution the way we've been tangled up with this place. Call it

11

an affliction. Sometimes you're born with something you don't know about, and it can be bad legs, a cough, a grocery store, or a place like this. Who knows what's waiting for a body. That's a pretty trunk the old goat is carryin' in."

"Yes, it's quite nice," said Madi, watching it go through the slab-iron open gates.

"Did they give you anything good, Leafy?"

"Leafy?"

The fat, middle-aged woman clapped her on the back. "It's an expression up here. Leafy. We have a lot of weather up here and we use it in expressions. Leafy is somebody . . . well, somebody sort of, yay-es, like you. Sort of light and flying. Like leaves. That's a pretty coat," she said. She fingered the material.

"Thank you."

"I'd like to see all you got in the trunk. I've seen most of the stuff the good folks have sent around. The barrels for the preachers and so on. This was an asylum here once. I was only a little girl then, but I saw the stuff from Boston. It was real foolish. Old silks. And the maniacs in there were freezing to death. But that's a mighty pretty coat."

"Thank you," said Madi.

"Look at the words graven above the gate," said the woman, holding Madi by the forearm, holding the pail of shelled peas in the other hand. Madi looked up at the stone arch above the open gates. There were no words.

"Can you read it?" asked the woman.

"I'm afraid not."

"It's obliterated," said Elvira. "You can see that, can't you?"

"I can't," said Madi; "it doesn't look as if there was anything ever written there."

Elvira squeezed her arm. "When I say there was something written there, there was something written there."

"I'm sure you know," said Madi.

"Of course I know. And I know the word *obliterated*. Would you have thought it?"

"I don't see why you shouldn't."

"I didn't go to school."

"I see. I wouldn't have known it."

Elvira laughed and stopped clutching Madi's arm. "Excuse me, Miss Brooks. I wanted to see if the jails had got to you much. They have a little, they have a little. You're afraid to tell me there's nothing writ up there and never has been. You

12

can tell I've done some wardening in my time. You can feel it in my fingers and tell it in the way I talk, even if I laugh when I'm doin' it."

"I could see nothing had ever been written there."

Elvira laughed. "Suppose I tell you what was written there and's obliterated."

"Please do."

Elvira laughed. "Getting some gumption, yays? Hah. What's writ, Miss Brooks, is 'All Ye Who Enter Here Abandon All Ye Hope.' " She turned and looked into Madi's face.

Madi said, "I've thought about doing so sometimes, but I never have."

Elvira put her arm around Madi's waist. "The people I'm fondest of remembering here are the ones that were just like that." She gave Madi a squeeze. "After a while we'll have some tea and I'll tell you about one of 'em. I never met her, though. I heard her screaming when I was a child, but I was too young to get in here. But I know people who saw her, so I can tell you something about her. Yay-es. But I heard her, and I think I saw her at the window once when we was standing way over there beyond where it was first cut over when it was an asylum. I met a lot of 'em, though, that was like you, careful, respectful, yet knowing their place if they didn't want it to be too hard, and yet waiting for a chance. I've known all this work almost all my life, so I can tell what's in your heart. I can tell. You're the kind that would gnaw through a wall for forty years, I can tell. I've spent all my life learning here. I used to be slop girl at the time when some of the folks around here still had the diem insane. Do you know what the diem insane were?"

"No, I'm afraid not."

They had walked into the prison yard. Neither the coachman nor anyone else was visible.

"Diem," said Elvira, "means day. I know lots of things even if I couldn't teach the children the way you're going to. Diem means day. For every day you kept a maniac, you got a certain amount of money. Folks around here who had some extra space in barns or root cellars or caves where you could put up chains could make a little money. You didn't have to feed them much more scraps than a dog. They were a lot more trouble than a dog because of all the noise. You whip a dog and he shuts up or you kill him. But if you killed one of these, you lost the diem. So you had to put up with a lot of noise. Oh, I guess I was about eight years old when I saw the

13

first one. I went over to do something, feed the man, I guess, and some more chores for Mrs. Halpern. She was one of the nicest women I ever met. They always paid their bills and were the highest in the community. If you sang in the choir, like I did, you always knew the Halperns were listening. Frugal. The farm was small and they made out very well. Mr. Halpern in the heat of the day had an attack and fell down. Something happened. The horses must of turned around and the plow took him right up the middle.

"I had somebody come over and ask me to help. They took him out of the field and did all they had to do, but I didn't watch the women coming over with the food, I did the chores. And that was my first maniac."

She threw back her head and laughed and squeezed Madi.

"He was in the root cellar. It was a small one so he couldn't stand up, full tall. He just got up as if I was a real lady. I was about, oh, eight, I guess. He stood up. I'll never forget it. He hit his head and I can remember some dirt coming down and settling around his feet. I had heard that he licked the frost off the stones when it was there.

"I knew his name. His name was Jim. There was a collar around his neck and he was chained to the wall. I had the bread and some meat and I was ready to throw it to him, which is what everbody did. You mustn't go close to them. But was a long time ago, and I was pretty in those days and he was looking at me, so I thought I would have some fun.

"I said his name. Just that. Yay-es. Just his name. Jim. And he looked at me and he pulled at the chain, I thought he was going to strangle himself. 'Jim, dear,' I said. I was very small, although I was pretty. A normal man would not have gone crazy. What normal man who goes to church would want a little girl? But the maniac did!

"Do you know what he did?

"I threw him his food, but he didn't even pick it up.

"'I'm Jim,' he yelled. 'I'm Jim.'

"He lunged at me. He tried to get me. He strangled himself on the chain trying to reach me. But he didn't make it. I stood away from him. I went right to Reverend Fostes and told him what had happened and they had the man taken into the yard and flogged. They didn't flog him on the back, they flogged him on the front. They only do that when there is some evil intent on the sex parts of a girl." She laughed. "I could see that whip work and I bet he didn't try to reach out from his chains and pull any girl in again."

14

They went through a small door set into the big door. The big door was a sheet of iron, four feet wide, eight feet high. "It's the most impressive door around here," said Elvira. "Do you know who put up the money for this place?"

"No, I'm sorry, I wouldn't," said Madi.

"A Jew. His daughter went insane. You can imagine why. He was a peddler, we saw him in the village for many years, and his father before him. Then they had a wagon, then a store. The usual Jews.

"This Jew's daughter went insane. He built her a cottage out here. My husband and I live in it now. We have for a long time. We don't have any children. God hasn't gifted us with that. We live in that cottage, though. We never liked Jews up here. Niggers either. We freed the niggers, but they're apes. As you know.

"We had one nigger here in the prison. He was a passion. He thought he was human and we were going to be nice to him. You should have seen it.

"What happened was we gave him the same thing what we ate and drank. He thought he was like us. Then we put a caustic in his next drink. It just burned his throat down to the belly. It took all that dark skin off inside him. He rolled around and I bet he didn't feel well. My God, that must have taken it off of the guts of him. It would have taken it off these walls. And this is the best stone you can find.

"It must have taken it off his guts. Do you know what I've done? You'll never believe it. I've given your room anything and everything a girl could ask. You'll see."

The stone floors echoed under their feet. From the small inset door in the huge front door they had entered a long, wide corridor. Doors were on each side but were closed and enigmatic. Ahead was an open door, made of iron. The hallway was damp and cold and a draft came from ahead of them. There was green mold on the walls and in several places there were rivulets of water running in green-gray patches of fungus. Madi did not know whether the chill in her came exclusively from that in the building or partly from the cheerful, almost happy brutality of the woman. The most uncomfortable thing about the woman was not only the cheerful malice and sadism but the fact that she emanated a real, very real sense of warmth and kindliness. She was doing her best to be nice. And to some degree she was succeeding, because Madi was not convinced that this woman was as horrid as she sounded. She was in an atrocious way misguided, but brutality did not seem native to

15

her. If Elvira had received Madi in the friendly way she had but had been speaking a foreign language that Madi did not understand, Madi would have been convinced that nothing passed Elvira's lips but pleasantries.

Madi's curiosity about the people she was to work for was at ebb. Curiosity must have a pleasant stimulation, usually, although morbid curiosity was sometimes as strong and frequently even stronger. But whatever morbid curiosity was part of Madi's makeup had been satisfied with a number of violent incidents. What she wanted now was to have an abeyance of curiosity so she would have an abeyance of information. She was already getting all the information she could consume, so what her benefactors were like did not at this point matter.

What mattered was that she was being struck with a wealth of sensory disaster. Her mind need not work, her imagination need not invent, and her emotions needed no stimulus. It was all here. The malignant, warm kitchen-kind of woman, and the seeming contradiction of the eroding stone walls, and the faint, deep smell that came from all sides, and the portentous sound of their steps in the corridor. Marching steps, echoing steps, prison-gaited steps. The lockmarch? Thum thrump. Thum thrump. Thum thrump. The walls implacably absorbing it and holding it in the deep, sour heart of the walls. And all around them inscrutable doors with pasts interred in them, of records of dead or maimed or screaming, with rooms where interrogations had taken place? Dusty rooms, perhaps, with old pain held in the atmosphere? Things were held in atmospheres. She was sure that you could walk blindfolded into a place like this and, even if there were warm fires around you and gentle voices, you would know that you were in a place where you did not want to be and where your heart could not breathe correctly.

She tried to make her steps quiet. She wanted to hush the place. Hush now, I know you, I have been here before, a prisoner myself, with all its debasements. I do not have to wake you, and you do not have to speak to me.

Suddenly she felt a tearless affinity. Her mother had died in jail, and she, Madi, had somehow wakened in jail. Her life prior to jail had been a dull, poverty-ridden attempt at respectability, a holding-up of the head among the other destitute in neighborhoods where it was better to dream than to think. Where it was better to burnish the mind with reasonless pride than step on the spittle. Where it was better to step on the spittle so you could pretend it was not there.

But in the jail every nerve, every pore, every heart of being had become sore and awake. She had become alive!

The kiss of pain, fright, and horror had let her eyes open and she had looked around with fear and anger, awake and alive.

They went past the open iron door. Elvira put out her hand and Madi stopped. On the long, wide, broad floor a shepherd dog was circling, catching rats and snapping their necks and putting the bodies in a pile. Elvira said, "That's General Grant. Cleaning up Richmond, or wherever it was. As soon as we make our presence known, all the rats will go away. But we have to stand here and clap our hands. But don't do it yet. You have to watch how good he is. Isn't it strange about rats? They come from down below. This prison's as deep as tall. And there's water down there, the cisterns. We don't use them, we use the wells outside. But they used to need them. The rats come up and take a chance with General Grant. Though they must know by now he's here. But if you just clap your hands, they go away. But you can't come downstairs or up or out there without clapping your hands because they might run up your skirts and give you a nip." She laughed heartily. "Nobody wants a nip like that. Look at the General fling them up and catch 'em and pile 'em.

"I sometimes wonder if that dog gets those rats in the very walls. Of course he can't. It's just all pure stone. But sometimes it sounds as if the squealing they're doing now happens in the walls themselves. It just sounds that way. They had to kill some people here during the war, and my husband had to help. He did a lot of the work around here, gardening and all, and still does. He put up the gallows out in the yard. I'd show it to you, but we used it for kindling. He did a good job, but there was a tall man here that had to be hanged. Tall? You never saw the like. So when he got hanged, it wouldn't work so well. He was standing on his toes. But Howard is a lovely man. A woman couldn't have better. When he saw that it wasn't going too well, he took the hammer out of his pocket and let the poor devil have it. It took him a few strokes, because Howard is sensitive and it bothered him to have to do it. Colonel never knew about it. We didn't bother him with details. When I drown kittens, I find myself the same way. I keep putting the bag into the spring and pulling it up again. I just can't bear to harm

17

anything." She clapped her hands and rats ran into holes in every direction.

The vaulted Gothic ceiling soared far above their heads. The dog came and lay panting against Elvira's shoe. She kicked him a little and smiled. "Good Granty." She pointed upward. "We don't have to worry about insects in the summer thank the Lord. See way up there, how dark it is? Bats up there. They just come swarming down and take every insect. Almost wish we had some over at the cottage. I don't take bites very easily, but Howard is fair-skinned and they just love him. I have to use the ointment all summer. Sometimes his face gets that blown up you wouldn't recognize him. But you don't have to worry about anything like that now." She laughed gaily. "Or rats upstairs, either. They scurry about the rotunda, but they have a deadline. They're driven below. I used to hear stories about the maniacs and then the prisoners down there, the way they got plagued by this and that. Water seeping and some kind of bugs that like to go into holes in the human body, and the rats. One story was really funny. It said something about who gets more afraid, the man or woman that bumps into the rat in the dark, or the rat. Which one was going to eat the other first." She laughed heartily. "Well, those days are over and for the better, I say."

The tiers of cells loomed above them, met by stone stairs and with stone parapets on all four sides. The black iron doors were closed, and presumably no one sat in any of the cells.

Am I? thought Madi.

What a silly notion. Of course.

"Where is my room, Elvira?" she asked.

Elvira pointed upward. "On the end of the first tier. Wait until you see how nice it is."

When they walked across the floor toward the stair, the floor made a booming noise. "There's a lot of space down there," said Elvira. "It's mysterious, but I'm too scary to explore. Anyway, there's enough around here that can give you the fantods without trying to go down there and look around. Did anybody ever tell you we have a ghost?"

"A ghost?"

Elvira threw back her head and laughed. She had a fat throat and a convulsive laugh. She wiped her face with her apron. "A ghost! Do you believe in them?"

"Not especially," said Madi.

18

There had been a time when she would have laughed at the suggestion of ghosts. But visualizing her mother in the numbered gray coffin turning round and round going into the sea had made her change her mind a little, because didn't people resent that sort of treatment, and was there not some sort of passion that could keep resenting it? Could that passion die completely? After all, in this very place already there was a design on the walls. Somebody had wept here, gone mad here, been mad here. It was a tangible thing. She knew that things had happened here. It was easy to know; she could see and she was being told. And she was sure that she felt it.

Did they weight the coffins so they would not turn and drift and turn and go away? Where? She remembered that her mother had had the gift of living place. She had been very patriotic. My country, my place. New Jersey, then Oregon, then New York. Mother turning over and over in slow sea cadence to China?

The thick stair left no echo as they ascended. But Madi could feel memory of the treadmill in her knees.

"You're a lot younger than me," observed Elvira, "but maybe you don't walk enough. I'm always exercising, and that's what keeps me young. You get out and walk around this place, it'll do you good."

"I'm sure it will," said Madi.

"The ghost used to live in your room," said Elvira. "I'll tell you about it when we have tea. I have a kettle in your room. It's a good story. She's supposed to still be here. There were some war prisoners that swore they saw her. She went insane because of being teased. By men. It's a caution what they did to her She was only sixteen. She only lived a year after she was in here. You have the room where she was chained. She was up here, not down below. Before she was seventeen, she was biting the walls. I painted over the marks. Then one day they went in there and found her dead. No reason. Dead. And she's been here ever since. And I believe it! It don't bother me any. I didn't do nothing to her. It don't bother me in the least. Howard and I are over in that cottage that was the first building here, the one with the Jew maniac, and we've never lost a good night's sleep. Not a good night's sleep. Here's your room."

With a flourish Elvira opened the iron door, not allowing it to bang against the wall. She made a gesture and Madi walked inside, half expecting the door to slam to behind her.

19

She stood inside the doorway and looked around. It was very pretty, considering. And much larger than she had thought it would be. It was quite the largest cell she had ever seen. It must have been at least ten by twelve feet and the usual nine feet high. A coal fire was burning in the stove and the fat belly of the stove was red. There was a cot with a red coverlet and extra blankets piled on a low, wide table at the bottom of the bed. The slanted, deeply inset, barred window had red and white curtains. Hanging on a hook above the window was a shutter and it, too, was red. The stone walls had been painted blue. There was a red and blue rug of the mosaic fashion on the floor. A varnished wardrobe was in one corner. Her humped leather trunk, presented by the good ladies of the Good Aid To Pariahs League was standing to one side of the wardrobe, ready for unpacking. On a table was a kettle and cups and a harbor that might contain tea. There was also a tin of biscuits. That table and the one with the ewer and pitcher held lamps. There were several books on the table beside her bed. She saw at once that one of them was the Bible.

Elvira had been standing beside her, chattering away with pleasure, but Madi had not made a word of sense out of anything she had said. She was speechless, and in effect brainless, because the room was a pleasant apparition. It was a very friendly dream, placed before her like a bubble.

She dared not breathe.

"I'll make tea," said Elvira, and proceeded to do so on the top of the stove, the pail of peas on the floor beside her.

They sat on the edge of the bed and had the tea and biscuits. Elvira said she would find a comfortable chair for Madi in the village. "But what I want to tell you about is the ghost. The story is known all over around here. She was as pretty as you can imagine. She was sixteen and working in the tavern. She was an orphan girl, yay-es. She never paid much mind to anybody, always walking along dreaming you might say. Then a man came into the tavern one night. The tavern isn't here anymore, not that one, burned down almost forty years ago. I was never inside it, never saw the way she was in there. But I heard about it. There was talk at table. She had two young swains that wanted her. One I can't remember much about, but the other was Alan Candless. He went for the law and got rich in Boston.

"But she didn't want Alan or the other one. She was just dreaming her life away. Hardly ever talked to anybody.

"Along came a handsome stranger," said Elvira. "Do you read any of those romantic novels? This handsome stranger came along and walked into the tavern, and she looked up, and something happened to her.

"I've never known anything like that, just read about it. Or Howard reads it aloud. It's mostly that way, Howard reading aloud. Most people I know just knew who they married all their lives. Never looked up and suddenly had something happen to them. But she did, according to it all. And he was a mystery!" She hugged herself deliciously. "A complete mystery. He rode up there on his horse and went in and had dinner and she looked up. She looked up and something happened.

"He stayed that night and went away. A long time went past and he came back again. Seemed to have money. Yay-es. I've heard horse traders talk, and they always say his horse was the finest they had ever seen. Yay-es. Every time he came back, she start to blushin'." Elvira laughed gaily. "I've heard about it all my life!

"Before, this room you've got here was the duty room during the war—it was the duty room for the guards on the tier, that's why it's large and has a stove. Before that, when this was an asylum, it was the room for the incorrigibles. It's bigger than the other cells, so there's room for whipping. You can't do anything else when they get incorrigible.

"There's still chains in some of the other cells, and down in the caverns, they're all there, but when this became the guard room during the war, the chains were pulled off the walls. But this was the whipping room when the girl was here, and she was in it most of the time. Couldn't do anything with her.

"Well, this man came a few times, and she was in love with him, and Alan Candless and the other one, whoever he was, got jealous. You can imagine. Then one day Alan and the other one and some of the other boys decided to wake her to her senses. They had one of the young boys who did some things around the tavern tell her that her swain, the mystery man on the beautiful horse, wanted to marry her. All she had to do was get ready. She had to make her a wedding dress and come up here on the hill—of course, it's lower than the hill road, but we still call it the hill, it used to be all trees and a big stream when the winter thaw came, there was a stream here and it was a cistern under the prison at one time, it begins up there on the mountain where there's sort of a quarry. All she had to do was come up here one

21

night wearing her wedding dress and he would pick her up onto his horse and ride off and marry her." Elvira laughed and pounded her thick thighs and tears came from her eyes, which she happily brushed off, and her voice rushed on. "She got some sheets and curtains and made herself a wedding dress. Yay-es! She came up here from the village all panting, I suppose, and the boys came out of the bushes and pelted her with pebbles and laughed and told her her swain had been hanged. Of course nobody knew whether he had or not, it was all funnin'. But she didn't have any sense of humor.

"That's why she went insane. Howard and I could never go insane. We can laugh about almost anything.

"I guess the poor girl had read too many of those romantic novels. As soon as she went insane, all she could talk about was gallantry. They say she helped prisoners escape from here during the war. Her ghost. That was because they were southerners. And that's what the man on the horse was."

Her eyes became brighter.

"There's a story, and I guess it's true, I heard my own father tell it. Men were teasing Sarah Winscott, that was her name, in the tavern one night when the mysterious stranger was there. Well. The stranger stood up and turned around and looked at them. My father said he had the softest voice ever. Just like silk. He said, "Any gentleman that disturbs the lady will have to see me in privacy that he will find unfortunate for him."

Elvira preened and shrugged, as if she had eaten something sweet. "In privacy that he will find unfortunate for him." She hugged herself.

Then inexplicably she stopped laughing and her face was pallid and her flounder-hands were tidied in her lap, and she was silent, her soft chin lifted, her light blue eyes fixed. She shrugged. "Howard likes all the romances. We only have a few books, but he does some borrowing, people that buy more." She shivered. "You won't find the nail marks on the walls where she tried to get out. They're painted over. There's lots of people around here that prayed for her.

"I guess I've done a lot of talking. Yay-es. I'm a gossip. They would of taken my tongue out times back. But it don't matter now. It don't matter. All ten of them that were supposed to have gotten out of here because of Sarah's ghost never were seen again. Just disappeared. Never seen again. This was supposed to be a prison that nobody could get out of, but one night ten of them were gone, and nobody ever saw them again.

"I haven't said too much. Yay-es. You'll see that. Because you'll hear more about it. Everything I've said and a lot more. You wouldn't be here if there wasn't a lot more."

The belly of the stove was somber red, and a little throb came from it. There was a black wisp around the edge of the black pipe that curved into the chimney. The curtains were parted by chill air and the bars showed like long teeth for a moment and the lip-curtain closed. Elvira's active body had become extraordinarily dull. Her flesh had fallen on her face and arms. It was as if her animation had been a frost that kept molasses stiff and strong, and now the frost was removed and her body was slipping to her feet.

"The colonel will be wanting to see you after a while," said Elvira. "He wanted you to get snugged in first. You just put some things away and have another cup of tea if you want it, and rest a little. Then me or somebody'll come to take you to the colonel."

She picked up the pail of peas and went out and softly closed the heavy iron door.

The colonel came to her. It was the most surprising face she had ever seen, made more so because she woke to it from an odd dream.

She only knew portions of the dream. Iron flanges that were steps up an inclined hill, and these, of course, were the steps on the treadmill. Then there had been crabs and she had been lying under a tangle of bent, rotted wood, unable to escape, and the crabs had been at the back of her dress, their claws at the entrance to her anus. The more she writhed, the deeper she became mired in the mud and then she had taken flight, whirling with her arms and legs around the squared-off edges of the gray coffin. Fishlike stars had bent around her and swam off with flickering tails. A horse with stars flowing from his mane had galloped by. And then a cold, soft sea had washed across her.

It had washed across her with a passion, with a wave force. Cold but strong. She had had the impression of resisting, of holding to something, of holding to herself. Then the sea had slid away, to return gently. Placatingly. A tide near the shore washing over her and embracing her. It was a deep, cold, soothing, imploring sea. And within it there was a mass of waving weeds, some of which stuck to her face. She tried to push them away and succeeded, but then there were more.

She was deep in the sea and very cold. But she was being

drawn upward, and there was a wind and it was cold and went against her cheeks. She was being borne upward to the surface and could feel herself emerging, cold and shivering, but still with maddening tendrils about her face. She thrust out at them and a voice said, "You're awake. You don't have to fight your dream any longer."

She opened her eyes to a cascade of gold, and inset in the flung gold like a jewel was a face with emerald eyes. He laughed and the long golden hair whipped her and the green eyes were peculiar stars.

"Colonel Harte Trace, at your service," he said. "I notice you drool a little."

"What?" Her hand flew with horror to her lips and she brushed at them. "I'm sorry."

His face was quite close. She wondered if he was going to kiss her. Fantastic notion. He probably had just been examining her features to see if there was a visible taint of the jail. Nevertheless, her face, which had felt chilled, began to warm, and he smiled and stood erect. "I'm sorry if I startled you," he said, "and I was not trying to steal anything from a sleeping lady. You looked so pale I wondered where you were. There are a couple of worlds, you know. The quick and the other." He was smiling and laughing all the while, a delightful mixture, although confusing. She could not tell at moments whether he was laughing at her or smiling with the smile that she felt come unbidden, but strangely welcome, to her face. He certainly was a handsome bizarre man.

Madi suddenly realized she was supine and rumpled and she sat up quickly. The colonel, who seemed to have his head near the ceiling when he was standing erect, said, "Ah, me, I haven't raped anyone since I marched with Sherman. It was considered a fairly decent gentlemen's sport at the time, but in these parlous times of peace it's frowned upon by a decadent, softening society."

She decorously—as much as possible—got her legs over the side of the bed and her feet on the floor and tidily arranged things while he stared frankly at her. "Before the war," he said, "I took a trip to the South Seas, and girls there don't have to take all the trouble you've just been taking. I was quite amazed to find that people had so much skin. I come from a family that bathes on a moonless night without a lamp."

She understood that he was treating her as an equal, and she was further warmed. And fortified. She did not stop the saucy flip of her long auburn hair.

"You are very flippant, sir."

"Also a liar." he said, standing, it seemed, almost to the nine-foot ceiling. He wore boots, breeches, an open tunic, a white open-throated blouse, and there was a black leather glove on his left hand. She wondered if his hand had been injured in the war. He did not seem to have the mate to the glove about him. His legs were straddled and the breeches were well-made. She could see the contained contours of something else. Her face got hotter and she lowered her eyes to the tips of his boots.

"What's wrong?" he asked, the laughter simmering through his voice. "You lower your head like a schoolgirl."

"You mentioned that you are a liar, sir?"

"Of course I am. What man worth his salt isn't? You can't be all you want to be or do all you want to do. There isn't time. So you have to lie the gaps between passion and the clock. Any man that doesn't boast and swagger is too humble to be a man, too afraid to be caught out. He isn't the kind of man who has what you were looking at a moment before."

He turned and went toward the door; her eyes were on his boots. But her eyes lifted to the hair flowing golden around his neck, and she came to her feet with fury. He had been treating her as an equal but too much as an equal You did not even talk to a lady this way. No man she would want would. And, more than anything, she was filled with disappointment. He had made her more than she had expected to be here and then had stripped her of it.

"You are insulting, sir! Is it because I'm a prison slut?"

He stopped at the door and turned. "Prisons don't necessarily contain people of that sort. Most people don't know that. They live their smug lives on the outside and don't care who rots in a place like this. It's too simple to say they deserve it. I told you I was a liar, didn't I? I didn't go with Sherman and do wild, urgent, therefore even excusable, things in war, like rape and burn. No, the long-haired colonel who stands before you was not an exciting man with pistol and saber. On horseback. The man you are looking at was the commandant of this prison, who held in cages many gentlemen, some of whom were a great deal better than he was. I did not ride them down, man to man, on horse. I made them walk a grain treadmill that ground their bread and gruel. I made them sleep on straw. They accepted it in dignity, for the most part. So that the least of men in this prison was me. That is always the case. The prisoners escape in one way or another.

25

They escape, they are released, they die. The sentence of the jailer is never ended."

There was no smile on his face and the flights of laughter were gone. She saw a landscape on his face that was bleak and unshadowed, like harsh light on bare stone. His voice was as flat and dark as the thick doors of the cells. "Come down to me when you compose yourself and receive your instructions."

She felt disturbed and looked for the slop bucket. It was nowhere to be found. But that box over there, with the neatly hemmed red-checkered square cloth. She lifted the box straight upward and there was the equipment. Elvira was delicate in some ways. Madi pulled the door shut. It was very heavy.

She lighted a lamp to come back to. She pushed the curtains aside and pulled down the shutter that had a ring and hasp to fasten. There was a scuttle of coal and she refurbished the fire. She rearranged the bed.

She stood in the doorway a moment, not surprised really to find that she was savoring the sight of her room. She was surprised that she wasn't surprised. But it was a room, and it was her own, and it had been done by a vicious woman who did not want to be. It looked very nice right now. There was some welcome in it. She hadn't been welcomed in a long time. Before the jail, she and her mother had never felt welcomed by the tenement rooms. Those had been more stained than this prison. And they had been prisons, too. And asylums, too, judging from the sounds. You had to wrinkle yourself down against the screams. What more bedlam could there be than free people who were not free but tried to pretend to be with drinking, fighting, and more?

She closed her door. It made her room look like the others. Closed, dead, forbidding, and empty, but she knew hers was not. The lamp was lighted, there was the stove and tea. And the scratching of fingernails might be on the walls, but it was beneath the paint of newness. And there were good clothes in the trunk that she had not hung in the wardrobe yet. It would be a pleasure to do so, despite the possible linty charity feeling of them. The colonel spoke about myriads of skin in the South Seas, but that was another place, legendary and invisible, and skin here that you could see was poverty, dirt, and shame.

There was slanted light from that side of the cell block, so that must be the west. Her shoes seemed to pound on the corridor beside the stone parapet to the floor below. Above her the vaulted ceiling was dying slowly along its riven groins. A wind tasting of dust and moisture was passing by.

She echoed in a profound loneliness to the floor below, finding that she must have been too preoccupied when ascending the stairs to notice the deepness of the indentures in the stone that had been made by hundreds who had passed this way before her. Each smoothed-out cup for her feet had been the shoe of someone thinking, breathing. Then alive, for a time, to leave here perhaps? Not to?

She paused at the bottom of the stair. She heard no scurry of dog or rats. She clapped her hands. There was no sound. She began to walk as silently as possible across the vast floor of the rotunda. Her imagination did not want her crossing to awake mystic sleep in the caverns that were silently sleeping beneath her. What had been there should not awake again.

She decided that the colonel would be in one of the rooms along the corridor that she and Elvira had first trespassed. That must have been the administrative part of the asylum and then the prison. She crossed the floor, holding her skirts tight against her, and in the center of the floor heard the thunder of the hooves of a horse. It was a wild running sound, and she could hear the shouts of a man. She wondered if the colonel had been lying the second time rather than the first, and that he was really a cavalryman and not a jailer. The stair she had come down had been on the east, so she ran across the floor to the side where the light and the sound was coming from. The exertion (or something else?) made her heart beat faster and she looked out, expecting to see the colonel and the golden hair charging around the prison yard. But it was not the colonel.

It was a smaller man, and because of the waving of the Confederate flag and the flashing of the saber, she could not see him very well. He was riding a magnificent chestnut horse and was riding it with skilled abandon. She hadn't seen a great deal of riding, but from what she had seen and what her mother had told her about the West, she knew she was witnessing a superb rider.

He was riding and yelling and waving the flag and the saber and holding the reins in his teeth. Madi stood there at the window and watched as he went around the building twice. She waited to see if he would come around again but he did not. The rebel yell was lost on the air and the thrumming of the hooves was gone. She stood there awhile in the window,

27

looking at the empty prison yard, smelling the raw earth that the charge had churned up. She had read a great deal about the war and she had heard about the fierce Confederate cavalry, but she had never seen or heard it, never quite imagined what the sight and sound would be like. It was a sight and sound of terror, fierceness, skill, and anger that chilled her more than lying asleep with bad dreams on the bed had done. She knew somehow that she had seen the kind of man she had never seen before. In a life that lately had had many chilling experiences, this was the most chilling of all. She did not know whether she would like to meet that man, or not.

He must be mad. But this was no longer an asylum. Or he had come back for some sort of revenge. But that was mad. The war had been over for more than two years.

Madi thought that maybe she was mad too. The rebel yell of the rider in the prison yard had chilled her again, but she hadn't been chilled with horror. There had been something gallant about his charge against nothing.

Gallant?

She remembered what Elvira had said about Sarah, the ghost. Sarah had spoken about gallantry, presumably southern gallantry in her throes. Was this rider another ghost? Sarah's gallant gentleman, returning to claim her? Madi laughed. It would have been history's loudest ghost, and although she had heard something about ghosts, she didn't expect they would churn up a yard on a beautiful horse.

She was still looking out into the yard when she heard a slither behind her and, turning around, she saw red eyes. She tugged her skirts, screamed, and ran.

Colonel Trace was standing in a doorway. "What made you scream, my crazy brother-in-law or something less dismal?"

"I saw a rat."

"If you looked into the yard, then you're right. What you saw out there was a captain of Morgan's cavalry. In other words, a rat. They were the only southern cavalry that would eat a widow's last chicken. Come into the office."

"Why does he do that?"

"He's living in the right place. An asylum. He doesn't know the war is over. He's attacking the citadel. The citadel is me. I have pity on him. I learned something about pity in my time here. I have feelings of guilt that stop me from going out with a pistol and shooting him down. Now, sit down."

28

Madi sat down.

He was very commanding. He was so commanding that she looked at him closely.

"I see you look at me suspiciously," he said. She hadn't known that he had been watching her expression. "What you think," he said, "is that I'm envious. I told you I was a liar. I wasn't the commandant of this hellhole until I was invalided out of the northern cavalry. I led a charge against Morgan. And we won." He grinned. "That Morgan, the lousy ... I went to school with him. I told him the best way to flank a cavalry charge was with cannon on one flank with a false drive on the flank. He remembered it. I didn't. I got the grape in my knee. But we won anyway. Morgan forgot something. He forgot that I told him that as soon as we were flanked by artillery, you flanked the artillery with the reserve unit, always posted to the flank of heaviest fire.

"Now, Miss Brooks, as to why you are here.

"I could tell upstairs, Miss Brooks, that you were insulted by my frank talk. I'm a soldier. But I'm not going to use that to excuse me. Instead, I'm going to tell you a truth that we learned in school. You treat a lady like a tart, and a tart like a lady. You're a lady, Miss Brooks, or you wouldn't be here. But if jail has made you feel like a tart, then you'll have to bear with it.

"The fact of your incarceration is the main reason why you are here. However, without education, and if you weren't a lady, you certainly would not have been acceptable.

"You are the complete schoolteacher here at this time, and for our purposes.

"You already think I'm callous, so I'll continue to be. The fact of the matter is that to find a schoolteacher for young children who could bear to live in a place like this would be almost impossible. You think I've insulted you by some of the blunt things I've said. That was intentional.

"You don't think for a moment, do you, that any teacher we could hire would have accepted my reference to sex organs?

"You have been calloused by jail, Miss Brooks, and it was necessary that we obtain someone who was. Oh, yes, you reared up and were angry but didn't faint. You didn't leave.

"Also, Miss Brooks, we don't want someone here who can just get angry and take a coach to some other place. I presume you know that you can't. You and your mother took

29

over your father's debts and they have to be paid. You don't owe them in this state, that's true enough. But your room and board here is owed to me. Your salary will, by agreement, be paid to the creditors elsewhere. If you attempt to leave here, I will institute a body attachment. After your other debts are paid, through the agreement with the people who have sent you here, your salary will pay for what you owe here, and then you will be free. I think I make myself clear."

"I am a slave."

"I don't think we use that kind of language in this state of the Union, Miss Brooks. I fought to abolish that sort of vocabulary."

"I would like to see your treadmill, Colonel."

"It's quite worn out, Miss Brooks. The gentlemen of the Confederacy needed a lot of bread."

He stood up. "We have an early dinner. It used to be the officers' mess. We will eat together here. All men, and women, I suppose, are created equal. No servants quarters. Take my arm?"

"I would very much like to," said Madi.

He looked down, and she hadn't taken his arm, and he uncrooked it and laughed and said, "You would have been excellent in the cavalry. We used to like to take their arms, too. I was so angry at Morgan that when some of his men put their arms up, we lopped them off at the wrists. In war you can't forget the fact that the enemy must be afraid. And also there is personal honor. I wasn't on the southern side, but I have some of their ideas. I can't imagine dying and knowing that somebody made a fool of me or tried to."

Madi could not find anything to say about that, not anything to disagree with. So as they walked the corridor to the mess hall she let him take her arm.

She would have liked—would have awfully liked—to have been able to say, "Mother, we won't take any of this nonsense. We absolutely won't. And that's that." When the constables showed up at the door, she would have spit. And if she didn't have enough spit, she would have found something else.

"Speak gently always to the little girls," he said.

She took her arm out of his. "And why wouldn't I?"

"The little girls don't know the world as we know it yet, and I would like them not to. I would very much like them not to. I have given orders elsewhere that they should not. And I give them to you."

"I hope you have lovely little girls."

"They are only mine in my mind. Because they should be. But they're not my daughters."

They turned right in the rotunda, to a long, narrow corridor that smelled of mildew. The colonel laughed as Madi held her skirts tightly around her. "Jail didn't get you used to the rats, I see."

"They didn't seem to have as much freedom as they do here, sir."

"They had more food than they have here," he amended. "More people, more food."

"Occasionally," she said, with spirit and memory.

"Yes," he said, "occasionally."

They came to a wooden door on the left that was open a crack. Light slid out, and warmth. The colonel pushed the door and it opened inward. There was a scraping of chairs as three little girls arose from the table, stepped back around their chairs and dipped knees under identical pinafores. Madi judged them to be about eight, nine, and ten. They seemed built to an identical scale for their ages. They all had light brown hair and features that had been made in a persistent womb. They stood behind their chairs gravely, hands folded before them, heads neither bowed nor wholly erect. Their long hair was tied with bows, that of the oldest with a yellow, the next with a blue, the third with a red. They shone with scrubbing. Their eyes and expressions were neither curious nor incurious. Light from a wide, burning fireplace shone through their ears. Their ears uniformly stuck out a little. They had a comic aspect, to which Madi reacted, but she suppressed it into a smile. They did not smile back. They stood like solemn little soldiers.

"Rest," said the colonel.

The change was abrupt and enchanting. The one closest to the door ran to it and slammed it shut. "That stinky hall. When are you going to do something about it, General?"

"When I tear the place down, Sergeant."

The other two were already at the colonel, climbing upon him. His face glowed in the light from the fire and the lamps. The third one climbed his back and put her legs around his neck. He hefted the other two to arms length over head, his flat palms on their bellies. This was obviously a trained performance. The girls arched their backs and put their arms straight forward and their legs straight back and the colonel began to whirl, and three girls were spinning in the air, screaming with delight. He whirled with such speed and

31

power that Madi was afraid one of the girls would slip or be thrown off. Then the whirling gradually diminished and the flying legs came down and his arms lowered the two who were high above and he squatted and the three of them, breathless, stood on the floor. They were panting, but the colonel wasn't. But Madi had noticed that he winced when he squatted and his face paled. The knee?

"Troops form," he said.

They rushed to the other side of the table and took their places again, and Madi realized that this was attention.

"I want to introduce you on this occasion," he said, "to your lieutenant. Her instructions are, of course, to be obeyed to the letter, because her instructions are by command of the officer in charge. That officer whom you have in the past moments violated with an unseemly abandon." They kept straight faces, but they worked hard at it.

"One of the things she is going to do," said the colonel, "is make you more firmly acquainted with the life history of nature's citizens, such as rats."

"Ugh," said the oldest girl.

"That will be enough, Sergeant," said the colonel. He glared.

"I introduce to you Lieutenant Madelaine Brooks."

They started to break ranks.

"As you were!"

They froze to attention.

"Dismissed."

They ran to Madi.

"I'm Liz." "I'm Marcy." "I'm Polly Ann. You're very pretty. Do you really know a lot about rats? Aren't they disgusting? Do you know what happened one day? Let me tell! Shep kissed Marcy! Ugh. He kills them and he kissed her. Don't say it! When she goes to sleep we're going to let him kiss her again." "I'll kill you!" "We'll do it!" "I won't let you, I never sleep. I only pretend." "You snore!" "I only pretend." "You lie." "I never lie!" "You don't do anything else, don't believe her." "I don't!" "You do!" "I'll slap, I told you, I'll slap!"

A silent man had come from the kitchen or the pantry, whatever it was back there, and had handed a drink to the colonel, who was leaning against the mantel and smiling indulgently. Over the mayhem at her waist and bust Madi was seeing everything. The creased—was it wistful?—smile of the colonel and the silent approach of the man with the drink on a small tray. The man looked young but wrinkled beyond

32

his age. His silence was not only a matter of not speaking or of walking without sound; it was an aspect of him. He was silent as a mist is silent. As stagnant water is silent. As color is silent. As the sky is silent. As time is silent, unless indicated by a clock. His face was cautious and watchful, and directed only toward the colonel. His eyes were doglike. His manner seemed to indicate a devotion—and an anxiety?

Without looking at him, the colonel knew he was there and reached out and took the glass and sipped, his eyes never leaving the animation of the three girls who surrounded Madi, who was making many formless replies to aimless questions. The silent man withdrew. An aroma of hot food was passing from the door he closed behind him. There was a din, and heat in the room, and Madi looked away from the colonel into three wellsprings of eager eyes that she could see wanted to adore her. They were hungry eyes, she saw then.

Not hungry for food, perhaps. The meal was a solid one of beef, potatoes, gravy, and canned tomatoes, but the girls touched little of it. Madi touched little of it either. She had seen eyes like theirs before, in the workhouse. The colonel ate magnificently. A vast calm was upon him. It was almost tangible. In his calm he ate meat and potatoes in a massive, unhurried way.

The girls' words had spun around Madi so swiftly and in such profusion that she felt dizzy. It was as if some constricting garment had been stripped from her when she realized that at a word from the colonel they had stopped their mouths, risen from the table, dipped their knees to her, kissed the colonel on the cheek, and gone.

"You saw that they need you," said the colonel.

"Yes."

"You'd better have something to eat now."

"I'm not hungry."

"You'll be all right in a moment. You were beseiged. I let it go on so you would see the depth of your responsibility." He knocked on the table and the silent man came in. "Brandy, coffee, cheese, and crackers," the colonel ordered. The silent man went away.

"Did you notice anything about their voices?" the colonel asked.

"No, not particularly."

"I'll tell you. Those are southern girls, from Mississippi. That's our home plantation there. Or the plantation of the rest of the family. I'm a northerner, by choice. All the women of

33

our family are taught to speak with a soft voice, a voice of honey sliding over the edge of a jar. And not just taught, they learn it by example. You didn't hear that kind of South in those voices, did you?"

"No, I didn't." She was intent and unconscious of the fact that she was not using "sir" or "colonel."

"The reason you didn't, Miss Brooks, is because for two years those children have been in prison." Her eyes flew open, but he waved his hand. "Not here, Miss Brooks, not a literal prison. A prison of neglect, which possibly is the worst prison a child could have. You won't have to draw mightily on your knowledge to teach them. They haven't had much learning in the past two years.

"Having been an active protagonist in jail yourself, as I was not, you might not have noticed that the voices of people in jail change. It does not matter what kind of jail it is, a jail of walls or one of conditions. Take the Negro, for example. Leave him alone in his cotton field, and his voice is soft and silky. You could almost take off your shoes and slide over a Negro voice. But just remind him that he's really in jail, give him a reprimand, frown at him, and his voice will go up high and come from the top of his throat.

"It happens to any person that feels bewildered or trapped. And being bewildered or trapped is the same thing. In the army, if you have a group of men in formation, at attention, on inspection, and you walk up to one of them and ask him a question, his neck muscles will constrict, and his voice will come out squeaky, no matter how brave he is. When you're at attention in the army, you're in prison. Punishment is only a small distance away if you try to move out of the trap of the way you hold yourself.

"What I want you to do for the girls, Miss Brooks, is not so much to teach them reading, writing, and arithmetic. That sort of teaching is only the excuse for having a teacher at all. What I want you to do is have the time and energy to listen to their bewilderment, and in listening to it make them come to a point where it's all been said, and when all is said, sometimes it's a lot easier. Your job is to develop southern voices again in girls who sound and act now as if they came from a prison slum of a northern city like New York or Boston."

The voice of the colonel had been so gentle and the fire, built up by the silent man, had been so softly radiant that Madi had relaxed and had found herself nibbling on cheese and crackers and taking sips of the brandy and hot black coffee. There had been cream and sugar, but she had not wanted it. She had wanted the stark flavor of the coffee.

Her eyes were heavy.

There were so many questions she wanted to ask, but she was too tired to ask them. And her fatigue took any edge off courage or brazenness.

She had told him that she would do what she could, and he had given her the warm accolade of telling her that he was sure her best would be excellent. "I did not blindly select you," he had said. "There are good women—and men, too, maybe, although I always distrust good men who are too interested in women in jail, and their welfare—there are good women in the city who do take a strong interest in people who find themselves in positions such as yours was. I could tell you a great deal about such people. I made a study of prisons in my long nights here, and I had visitors who did their best to enlighten me. I read and I listened during the long nights when this place groaned with souls in torment. The soul is supposed to be, in many ways, independent of the body, Miss Brooks. But that doesn't seem to be so when prisoners sleep and are free inside themselves, against the rigors of the mind, and try to find escape, only to discover that the body itself is a dungeon from which there is only one escape."

Everything was so soft and luminous, the fire, the brandy, his voice and the light on his long golden ringlets. His green eyes were somber but tender. The fragments of broken glass in her emotions were coated with hazy peace.

"People who go to jail or prison," he said, "undoubtedly feel, for example, that solitary confinement is a great evil. You, of course, did not have to be asked if you wanted it."

"No, I was not asked."

"No," he said, "because you did not commit a real crime. People who spend too much money, so that others suffer for it, do commit a crime of course. It's a form of stealing without courage. But you did not yourself commit that crime."

A momentary awakeness and fire came to her. "And neither did my father!"

He said nothing, and she felt the loyal anger melt away in her tiredness. Poor father. Yes, he had gotten willfully into debt, but it must have been born in him. He didn't seem capable of doing it any other way.

"The jail is a very promiscuous place, isn't it, Miss Brooks?"

"Yes."

"There was a time, Miss Brooks, when children like those you met tonight lived without segregation with adult male felons. It still happens, as a matter of fact. But the Quakers and the Seventh Day Adventists are destroying that. Privacy, Miss Brooks. Even when alone it's sometimes hard enough for a man to give fresh air to his heart. Much less when his legs are entangled with a filthy person that only fire—not even water—could clean."

The warmth from the fire and the brandy, and his soft voice, was soporific.

"Miss Brooks?"

She felt herself picked up and carried. His hair moved back and forth against her cheek, merged with her own hair. She could not tell which was which. It was cold in the corridor after the warmth of the dining room. She saw the identical faces of the children, graduated only as to age. What was behind those pristine foreheads and stuck-out ears with the firelight glistening through them? Another sameness? She had not been able to tell.

Her hand was against his breast and she felt his beating heart. Her limbs felt weightless, her mind a slow, emptying pool. She was being drawn out of herself and going away. It was a very pleasant sensation and she had had few. It was corrupt indulgence, and perhaps he would think her weak and send her away. Did the brandy make her giggle?

The rotunda danced above her, endlessly dark. She did not hustle her skirts against her over the drumming of the rat arena. They could not get her now.

She was floating up the stairs, hearing a soft regular breathing, and his arms were smooth ships on which she sailed. And she was a fool who had drunk brandy, or his voice, or fire, or a fool who liked prison? This prison? Shadows, dark, soft, lingering traces of light past, windowed? Her bed? She was lying down. Was he undressing her? Her shoes. The ringlets touched her face. His mouth? A door closed. She had blankets over her and in the dark the stove was a dim red horizon that she saw before darkness.

It was a febrile feeling. Madi came half-awake. The sensation of the clinging limbs was tawny. Madi had opened the shutter and the moon was enough to show her the face of the oldest girl, Polly Ann. It was disturbing that it was Polly Ann who had managed to come to her bed. If Polly Ann wished to, then perhaps the others had wished to. Then Polly Ann had used prerogative. Force? Madi had seen that in jail.

The girl was asleep, and she did not wake her. If there was some force being used for various reasons, she would find it out in due time, and nothing could be well served by waking the child and doing it now.

Light was coming in when Madi woke. It was not full late October light, so she knew it was still decently early. She was alone in the small bed. Had she dreamed the girl had been here for solace? Had she dreamed the rest, that the door had opened and the colonel had come in and stood a moment above them and then touched both their heads? Had she heard him say, "There are three girls." She did not know. Imagination, dream, fatigue, the strangeness—all could have consorted to make things seem real that in no way were. But she had distinct, if distant, impressions and she thought she could yet feel Polly Ann's clinging body. The arms and the legs had been intense, soon relaxed, warm and skin-touching.

But she really did not know.

She sat up in bed and rubbed her head. Her throat was dry and she needed the slop bucket. Cold air folded around her shoulders and she lay back and pulled the covers up again.

She lay there assimilating courage for the pulling-together of herself. Better to lie here awhile and suffer a small amount. It wasn't large if you kept movement down. Better than stepping out into that cold right now.

Curled up, she started to fall asleep again. There was a strong tug at the door and Elvira's voice said, "Drop your cocks and grab your socks."

Madi sat up. Elvira's boisterous face was grinning. "They used to say that when the prisoners was here."

"Oh."

"I have some hot water, if you want to wash."

"Thank you."

"Do you think I'm vulgar?" said Elvira.

Madi's mind felt clear and strong this morning. Clearer and stronger than it had been for a long time. She knew that there was a need for her here, and she knew that although the colonel had in a way declared her a prisoner, he hadn't meant it. She felt that she could walk out of here whenever she might feel like it. And she felt that she didn't want to. It

37

was wonderful what an impression of freedom of choice could do.

"Yes, I do," she said.

"You think I'm vulgar?" said Elvira.

"I think you attempt to be."

Elvira put her hands on her hips and stared at her. "Getting pretty uppity for the first morning, aren't you?"

Madi wondered whether she had misjudged Elvira. She had thought she had seen a vicious, good-hearted woman with a sense of humor. Or was she only a termagant whose mouth could not be controlled because an inner acid made the mouth run and corrode anything in its way.

She was sorry she had spoken in the way she had. It wasn't necessary to have an enemy here so fast.

"I got drunk last night, and whenever I do, I get uppity."

"Who did you get drunk with?" asked Elvira, leaning forward, hands on hips, and leering.

"The colonel didn't get drunk," said Madi. "I'm not used to it."

"You don't look as if you're used to anything," said Elvira. "Jail or no jail. Now, get out of that bed. I told Howard I'm bringing you home for breakfast, and he's going to make it while I'm gone. He used to do lumbering as the cookie, so he can make breakfast. You're a weakling, or you wouldn't be hugging those covers like that. I'm taking you out of that bed, sister, and you're getting washed and dressed."

"Elvira, no! Let me collect my wits!"

"You should of collected them. Yay-es."

Outside of the walls, they walked through a field of clover. A gigantic gray cat reared up with a rabbit in its mouth that was almost as large as it was. "Scat!" said Elvira to the cat. "Jail didn't do you much good." she said to Madi. "Scared of a thing like that? You should of lived my life. You'd eat the rabbit, cat and all, and not even worry about a toothpick."

She took Madi by the arm. "Those cats were brought here for the caverns, to take care of the rats. After a while there were more cats than rats. Or the cats were worse. Then they got dogs to take care of the cats. Down in the caverns the rats got the dogs. There's only that one dog now. The cats went outside and the rats came in. I don't understand it, but maybe my husband can tell you how it is if you want to know. He knows all about that kind of thing. We have the prettiest cottage. It's behind those pines over there." She sighed sentimentally. "It's the first place here. For the Jewish girl, as I told you. When you see it, you wouldn't believe that all this and everything that happened here was because a girl's father wanted her to be insane in a place where she could look at pretty things and nobody would hurt her. But he started it all. He got the asylum and prison here by caring so much about her and then trying to care about other people. And, soon there were the whippings. I never saw Sarah whipped, I was too young. But I had an uncle who did. He didn't whip her. But he saw it. She was naked right down to the waist. That wouldn't happen nowadays. Not that. And around her feet was a pool of blood. She hadn't even reached her seventeenth birthday. But what're you going to do?"

Elvira was panting as they ascended the small slope of cut-over ground that surrounded the prison for two hundred yards on all four sides. Then they came to a steeper slope that led into the pines and Elvira labored with her hands on her thighs. Her cheeks were flushed purple. "I have a lot of aches and pains," she said, "and I think this helps me. All the straining. Course you can't always tell. Maybe it's the other way. Howard does as little as possible. He's responsible for some things around here. Keeping the fields cut over, keeping the fires going. He don't do that too well. There's supposed to be five fires, but when you got here yesterday, there was only two, and one of 'em, yours, I made myself. Howard says there's just so much water in a glass." She was panting and wheezing, and talked in between. "Howard's full of good sayings, especially when they're good for him. I've heard tales of maniacs that was chained for forty years and weren't young when they got started at it. They kept the water in the glass all right. Wonder what they thought about? Hard to imagine. See those busts of colors on the leaves. Call 'em busts of colors here. We don't always stand on ceremony with words. Makes talkin' easier.

"The children are little scamps, ain't they? Yay-es. You'll find out they ain't what you think. Not to my mind, they ain't. And I'm sure your mind is about as normal as mine, considering what you've been through." She stopped and wheezed and adjusted some complicated structure of undergarment or body, or both. The color of her face was shocking. "Smell the fall?" she asked. "People dying don't smell that way, I can tell you. There's a graveyard over there past that little uprising. We'll peek at it. A real pretty little yard, with nice white crosses. Howard's supposed to keep 'em painted, but he don't always. Don't suppose it matters. Those that are left here, their people didn't want. The maniacs and the soldiers.

"We can't take more than a peek because she's in there this time of day. Has all these papers, checking all the graves. There's quite a few graves, and she's going to check on them, even the empty ones. She wants every grave around here accounted for, even mounds that might not be graves, or even graves that are supposed to be real old."

She stopped again, moving and talking, and her pleasant, discolored, peasant face was sharp with curiosity, humor, and intelligence. "Girl," she said, "you learned not to ask too many questions, didn't you? You learned to keep your mouth shut, huh? Yay-es. When you're poor and when you're in jail, you learn that." Her alert eyes were on Madi's face. She laughed. "But you got the fire in you, haven't you? I can see it. I can see the fire in that tight little chimney of yours. But you know how to keep that little mouth shut, don't you? Most of the time. Until you get real mad and proud. They didn't take all of the proud out of you, did they?"

She laughed, coughed, and spat. "Forgive that," she said. "That's something we usually stand on ceremony on up here, but it can't be helped if you've got the sickness. I don't think I do, there's no blood in it. But I've been chilled a lot, a lot. That's a cold place you're living in. If I spent all my time in it, I guess I'd be a lot worse."

Her eyes were beaming with kind malice. "You haven't asked any questions since you've been here. You've just taken it from whence it comes. Isn't there any burning curiosity in you? Aren't you fairly sizzling, wondering?"

Madi questioned herself and was disturbed to find that she did not have a burning curiosity. The honest knowledge frightened her. She had lost a normal human endeavor. The endeavor to know, to confront, to use. Was she on the first step of the ladder to becoming a vegetable, like so many she had seen in the jail and in previous slum squalor?

"You're afraid to know anything, ain't you?" said Elvira, putting her cold, sweating hand on Madi's. "Afraid you might lose the fire and the food and the dignity of being a teacher. Maybe you're no Sarah. Do you know what? Maybe Sarah wasn't crazy. Maybe she was just different than other people. Nothing was good enough for her, unless her spirit said so, and she'd druther be whipped than grateful for her portion."

40

Confused, ashamed, Madi lowered her eyes, but as soon as she saw the aggressive, pointed-apart tips of the older woman's shoes under the hybrid skirts colored naturally or with living itself, she felt shock at the base of her spine. She thought that she was being degraded for some purpose this woman had, some alien hostility that she had never encountered before and could sense but could not understand.

She raised her eyes and was glad with the way they met the eyes facing her. She felt her eyes direct, honest, keen, and not conciliatory.

"I've been afraid of my portion. I've been ashamed of my portion. But my mind has never bent to kiss a foot."

The face before her was still crimson and blotched, but it was quiet and watchful. The woman held a soft but capable hand to her still-rapid breast. "Pride," she said. "Pride. Yay-es. And you're proud of your pride." She raised a fat, surprisingly long finger. "Sarah, had pride, yay-es. Wasn't that it? Not being insane, being proud, so stubborn she couldn't take it off and throw it in a corner. It was her skin and got her whipped!

"And the colonel, the colonel!" All the candles of her personality, whatever it was, burned in her eyes at one time. "Pride! You have seen it! With his hair and his belief in himself. Least Howard don't believe in himself. I'd smash him with a skillet if he did."

She paused, and her body, which had been upraised and fierce with a strong (envious?) passion shrank into its folds of conspiratorial flesh, and she was a fat, mocking sneak, who put a fat finger to her lips and said, "I'll show her to you. She isn't like you, or the colonel, or Howard, or me. There is no pride in her face. There isn't anything. Anything we know up here in New England. She's like a stone. No, not like a stone, a stone don't do anything. She's like ... she's like one of the machines in the prison, the treadmill. I used to watch sometimes when they were on the treadmill, the way it went on and on. They'd faint and fall off, one broke his neck, another his arm. But the treadmill was always the same. Always the same."

"It's broken," said Madi. "It changed too."

Elvira grinned, so widely this time that she showed irregular teeth and the indentation above her gums. She nodded wisely. "Machines get broken," she said. "Machines get broken. Sometimes quicker than you'd expect. But come on, Howard will be getting angry, and I want you to see her."

They stood on a knoll under a color shower of red and golden oak. Beneath them was an unkempt oblong of graves, with an unmortared low stone wall around it. In the center of the graveyard was a kneeling woman, lithe, with long shiny red hair, a very deep russet color.

She had a board of papers and was intently examining a cross, her back to them. She was wearing trousers, deep green, boots, and a masculine jacket. She was a picture of careful patience. She sat back on her heels and wrote something. Her back was long and defiant. There was something about her posture and her auditory attitude that was immutable, as if no sudden clash of sky could alter her purpose. Madi was conscious of an impression of power. The woman's hair burned on her head; and she arose with a graceful exhibition of easy muscle, and went to the next cross.

"Why don't you ask who she is?" asked Elvira.

It swept over Madi that she did not have to ask who it was.

Many things had penetrated her in the brief time that she had been here. Sensitivity had become dim in the months of the jail, in order that she should not too clearly perceive that her mother was suffering too much and dying too soon. There had been nothing that she could do about it, and therefore she had become asleep in part, unaffected in part, as, perhaps, soldiers had to become in war in order to survive and fight. The strength of her tenderness and perception had had to sleep within her so she would not scream or hopelessly rebel. She had never wanted, and would not want now, a rebellion within herself as wild as Sarah's, to no avail but further shame and whips and nails on walls. And yet there was something to be said for Sarah's position; she had not crawled into a hole, to lose the most precious part of being a human being—awareness of what was around you. There was no pastoral for a beast in the blinding orgy of fall New England, but even a nonrunning, nonbeautiful human cripple could perceive it.

She, Madi, had become to some extent an animal, in allowing only the feelings, whether of the mind, the mouth, the hope, or the fingers, to hold sway in her.

And the most repulsive part of all was that she had been swayed most by the hope for fire, its warmth, and friendship, and gratitude for clothing, and a kiss from a handsome man, and to be benevolent to children and feel them love, and to eat at one end and find the adorned slop bucket with the other.

She did not have to ask who that woman was because that woman was so intent on what she was doing that she would neglect children. The woman was the mother of the children.

That woman was checking graves of all characters, those in graves, those removed, and those possibly buried elsewhere.

She had a board of information on the graves, and the war had been over for two years, so she had been searching for a long time. And the trail had led to here. Therefore, there was a very important grave that she was looking for. The grave of her husband.

Since the children did not belong to the colonel, but were obviously in some way the colonel's, the colonel was their uncle.

Since the colonel's brother-in-law in Confederate uniform rode around the inside of the walls of the prison on a chestnut horse and waving a saber, the brother-in-law was this woman's brother, and this woman was the colonel's sister-in-law—and the man she was looking for was the colonel's brother.

And Sarah Winscott, the ghost, in love with a southern gentleman, and a resident ghost here, had led ten southern gentlemen to freedom, but they never reappeared. So Mrs. Trace, down there in the graveyard, had been following it up all along the way, until there was no other thing to believe except that they did not leave this prison.

And the colonel?

The colonel was here to see if they were found, or the colonel was here to make sure they weren't.

And what was she, Madi, doing here? Was she here because, as the colonel said, only a person who had been subjected to prison could stand living in this place? That had seemed as right as good bread until you considered the fact that except from the historical standpoint and what might be going on here, this was an interesting, not unpleasant, place and many an adventurous young woman might have taken the job if importuned to do so.

No, perhaps it was not merely the fact of Madi's prison, or, rather, jail, experience that had been interesting to the colonel—perhaps it was Madi's expected fear of knowing anything that had been interesting to the colonel.

Madi looked at Elvira carefully, in profile. Elvira was watching the woman. Madi saw the hanging chin, the poached-egg side of Elvira's face, the avidity in the watching. Did Elvira know something that she wanted Madi to know and was trying to direct her to in the challenges and the indirect conversation? Or was she only a creature of instinct and prescience, a woman who knew pertinent things one moment and lost them the next, a woman who suspected only for the enjoyment of talking about it before a cup of tea or a fire?

Elvira turned to her. "Now you've seen them all except for the kitchen niggers they" —she pointed at the woman in the graveyard—"brought with them."

"I see."

"Her brother's down there in the caverns digging while she's up here doing this. He's got a lot of real dirt over him. Howard says if they want to use so much energy, they ought to make money at it."

The color in Elvira's face had subsided to some extent and her smile was as kind as Madi had ever seen it, and her eyes were as watchful, seeming to take in Madi's features one by one, as if trying to find something. Something to cling to, something to believe in, something to tell to? There was a wistful waiting in her expression that Madi found challenging.

"Is there anything more you want to tell me, Elvira?"

Elvira leaned toward her. "Howard's probably very mad by now. Keeping that breakfast going."

Madi said, "Is there anything else you want to tell me?"

"About the colonel? Even the kitchen niggers, peeking out, know the colonel likes you. You're out of it, dear. You might get the colonel if you try."

Madi was sure the woman was testing her out.

"I know you want to tell me something else, about what is happening here, and I can assure you I'll do everything possible to help."

Elvira's face went blank. "Help to do what?"

"Why, to find out what's wrong here?"

Elvira frowned. "What's wrong here? Nothing's wrong here. Everything's the way me and Howard want it. It won't be long until all of you are gone. This won't be a prison again. It was an asylum at first because it's way out in the woods and people couldn't hear 'em screaming, but it's different now. They have them in closer, with a lot of doctors. And it was all right as a prison for soldiers, so if they escaped, there was noplace to go. But it won't be used for a regular prison. A regular prison has to have a place to sell the work the prisoners do. They have to earn their keep, don't they? A regular prison wouldn't work out here. No, all you people are going to go away, and then Howard and I will be all at peace here. The colonel told us that, and he knows all about such things."

"I see."

"Haff!" exclaimed Elvira. "You say you see. You don't see anything! Those people"—she pointed to the woman in the graveyard—"think the colonel killed his brother. They know better; they're just desperate. They're at the end of the line, and they have no sense. Like Sarah. She would never accept the end of the line. And they won't either.

"But they know the colonel didn't kill his brother. The colonel couldn't kill anything. That's why he was sent here. He's a poet. I don't know whether some poets can kill people, but the colonel can't. He led an attack against some southern general, and retreated druther than kill anybody. So they sent him here. Then he wouldn't kill the rats, then he wouldn't kill the cats. So they killed each other and the dogs. When he was first here, this place was so overrun you couldn't walk around without falling over something biting you.

"The only reason the colonel lets that dog range around in there is because of the children. If a drop of blood was drawn out of the children, the colonel would fall on the floor in a faint.

"We've tortured Howard long enough, so let's go eat like lumberjacks."

"You're a pair of bitches!" said Howard.

He was not the silent man.

"You call her that because she was in jail!"

"You wasn't in jail and I call you that!"

"You put that stuff on the table and shut up!"

"Who made your mouth so wide? I wasn't married to you then."

"You ——"

"Shut your face and sit down. Us cooks don't like interference! And now you hear me and shut up and sit down!" His twangy voice subsided. "Young lady, we're proud to have you for breakfast. Never mind my wife, she yells and screams, but she has some nice pores here and there. She tastes like rye bread. You look as though you have a small stomach.

45

But that can't be any excuse. Mark me! You're a lumberjack this morning. Think you can make it?"

"I'll try," she said. He was tall, with big hands and a smooth face. He moved around indolently. A gray cat jumped on his shoulder. "Get off there!" he said, and the cat jumped off. Howard stood in front of the stove, holding out a big hand with a big spatula. "Sausage, flaps, biscuits, beans, but no cook ever made 'em like me." He turned firmly to the stove. Madi saw Elvira watching him with an adoring smile.

It was a pretty house that Elvira and Howard lived in, so pretty that Madi would have loved to have thought about it for herself and someone, if she hadn't known that this sweet germ of a house had spawned the stones of the prison.

It was a strong cottage, with small windows. Unless you had known its original purpose, you would not have thought of it as a jail. But having been in a jail, and now a prison, and knowing what this cottage had been for, Madi could see its restraint.

There were a lot of lovely windows, but they were very small. Only a small child could have gotten out of any of them. Yet Madi was sure the house was filled with sunshine during the day and moonlight when it was available. The house was sort of a combination place, a child's house, a cottage, a doll's house, a prison.

It was tight, warm, cozy, forbidding. Her pleasant breakfast hosts, the fire, the breakfast did not take away the fact that it would be hard to escape from this small, sweet house. She was glad when Elvira opened the door to her and she was able to walk (home?) to the prison in the small, chill, flaming morning.

ᴖᴄ CHAPTER II ᴐᴖ

HOWARD HAD GOTTEN THE SCHOOL supplies on a trip to Peeksmith. Madi would never forget the shadow that had crossed the colonel's face when she confronted him with the fact that school could hardly be held without some basic equipment.

She hadn't intended to start school right away but had decided on the Monday following her arrival. In the meantime she would get used to the children, the people, the place, and herself in her new role. Although she had found that the children had had irregular schooling over the past two years, and frequently none at all, she had assumed that supplies had been obtained and stored for her and their use. It was a natural assumption to make because of the authoritative and concise manner of the colonel when he had initially given her her instructions. And, of course, he was a military man, quite used to planning, and this would be true despite what Elvira had claimed about his inability to kill.

She had looked at him brightly in his office on Monday morning. The silent man was doing the work of an orderly, with mop and pail. She had noticed over several days that the silent one performed several of the functions that she understood certain enlisted men in the army did. He took care of the colonel's horse but not the other horses. He sat at a desk in the colonel's office and made out reports of some kind. He was able to type. He was obviously the steward of the kitchen, and if you wanted to see the colonel about something, this man, if he was present, apparently wished you to speak to him first. And when you did, he would wordlessly turn to the colonel and lift his brows in question, and the colonel would reply, "Very well, Jenkins," in a fond but distant way.

It was almost a theatrical performance, a travesty of the regimen in a military office as Madi could imagine it.

"Colonel?" she had said, standing before his desk.

"Please sit down, Miss Brooks," he had said. His golden ringlets were sparkling on his shoulders. His green eyes were alert and pleasing. His mouth was wide and quite dry. She had over the days become more and more sure that she had felt that dry mouth against hers. Against her cheek. Against her forehead. Was this a hallucination, one she conjured up for herself for some reason? In her cell, her room, it was a simple enough matter to conjure almost anything. Her mind was rife with fantasy when she lay there between the soul-twilight of waking and asleep. She knew full well that there were two essential strong elements in her nature—one, the ability to sort and recognize fact, and the other the ability, or the snare, of growing apparitions, romances, horrors on walls, including the wall of her own brain.

What Elvira had said about him was not distressing to her; rather, it appealed to the romantic side of her nature, and did so more easily because of the torment there had been in her life through people who did not seem to care whether pain was inflicted. His sensibility, combined with Elvira's information that he was a poet, made him a figure that appealed and yet was tragic.

In his own way he would be tormented too, and probably far more than she, if he were playing the farce of being a brave long-haired soldier, at the same time knowing he was nothing of the kind and constitutionally incapable of being. And what of the feelings of a man who could not kill but was suspected of killing his own brother?

"Sir," she said, "I'm afraid I can't find the school supplies, and Elvira has no idea where they are."

He had been broadly and indulgently smiling at her. The smile did not fade, it was fixed to his face. But the cold shadow slid under it and froze it, so that it was as much a sunny smile as a glare on ice.

He turned his head slowly to look at the silent man. Madi's eyes followed the turn of his head, and she saw the silent man standing there with a stricken look on his face. The kind of look a person would have, Madi thought, if someone he cared for had suddenly had his face ripped with a broken bottle. She wondered where she had gotten such a horrid notion and then knew it was from a composite of several scenes she had witnessed. The face of a man whose friend had slipped and fallen into a pit in the jail compound while she had watched from a window. It had been a drainage pit, filled with slime. And the colonel's face as he looked at Jenkins resembled the face of a woman who had slipped on

48

the treadmill and her face abruptly winced, with a combination of the same emotionless expression she had had and the onset of the pain she had just begun to feel. And she remembered the fight she had seen—if that it could be called—when a man had without warning lashed out at a face before him, an unaware, smiling face that suddenly was cut with jagged glass.

"Jenkins," said the colonel sternly, "did you forget or countermand that order?"

Jenkins shuffled, but his gaze contained something like triumph as it turned to Madi. He nodded yes, and then nodded no.

"That will be all, Jenkins," snapped the colonel, and Jenkins picked up his bucket and left the room, trailing his mop.

"Goddamn inefficiency," thundered the colonel, hammering his fist on the desk. "I've had that man with me ever since the army, and I'll probably have him the rest of my life. But he isn't army, goddamnit. Used to be a good man, have to hand him that. One of my sergeants, one of the best. But something happened to him the night he got shot. In the throat, you know. Has never spoken since. I dropped everything—we were in the midst of an attack—and held him on my lap, holding that wound closed until we could get a surgeon up. Saved his life. It's made him like a dog, and you can't kick a dog away. But the goddamn inefficiency. If you want something done, you've got to do it yourself. Always found that out when I was doing staff work. Don't delegate it to the staff, damn it all, I told myself. Do it yourself and then you know it's done!"

His voice calmed; he visibly composed himself. "Now, Miss Brooks," he said, pulling forward paper and pen, "let's get this done."

A terrible compassion filled her and made her wince. She wanted to stand up and bend forward and kiss that bowed, magnificent golden head.

At the same time there was a revulsion. She was sure he was hiding behind Jenkins—as perhaps he had needed to do before?

When she left the office after they had completed the list of things for Howard to pick up in Peeksmith, the colonel had followed her to the door and his smile gave her a shock. It was a wry, dashing smile. "You're very quick and precise," he said. "Maybe they should have had women in the cavalry." It was a desperate, gay, gallant, ironic smile. "Thank you," she said, and hurried away.

She had looked into that smile before, but it had not been on the colonel's face, not this colonel.

She had first seen that complex look last Saturday afternoon. In the morning she had accompanied Howard, Elvira, and the children into the village to pick up supplies and mail. The children had gotten candy and Howard had excused himself and had returned neatly after the shopping was done with the raw smell of whiskey about him. "Incorrigible," Elvira had said.

Howard had slapped his thigh. "You know what she wants to do to me, Miss Brooks?"

Elvira threw back her head and laughed, and said, "Don't you say anything more in front of the children."

"No, no, Viry, I wouldn't do that, wouldn't do that!" He laughed and slapped his thigh. "The colonel would raise hell if those children knew what you'd like to do to me. Incorrigible, uh?"

The sound of the whip. "What can you do?" Elvira had asked, concerning the incorrigible maniacs. Howard had had enough drinks to laugh all the way home, and Elvira reminded him to hold his tongue and to manage the horses.

After lunch, which Madi shared alone with the children, the children went off to their quarters for their hour rest period, prescribed by the colonel. The noon meal here was not dinner as was usually the case, but was a light repast. This was also prescribed by the colonel. Sometime during his war career, he had been an inspector of factories that supplied field rations in cans and material for cavalry units. Because it was inconvenient for factory workers to eat the big meal at noon as had always been done on farms and in crafts and was still done in the army, the workers had brought small meals with them and then had had their large meals at night. The colonel had observed that these factory workers were more efficient for the rest of the day than soldiers or the field workers he had known.

"It's a lot of work, Miss Brooks," he had said one evening, "to digest a meal. And you can't do two jobs at once if you want to do at least one of them right. In most circumstances, the work is in the daytime, so it's best to do your work on food at night."

"That's quite revolutionary, sir," she said.

"I can't take credit for an original thought, Miss Brooks. couldn't help but see that it's best. Sometimes some thing prove themselves. A man in a factory can't pick up and go home for dinner, so he waits for it, tiding himself over, and finds he works better, and the old habit was of no benefit."

Sometimes his rhythm of speech reverted to the South.

"I've given a lot of thought to a number of things," he said. "I guess my main concern has always been making a man less of an animal than he needs to be. Trying to purify the race, I guess you might say. I don't mean keeping it pure of Negroes, I've never taken them into account. I'm not sure of my feelings about them. I don't want to be because I can't understand what I feel about them. And I don't think I ever will be able to. The reason is this, Miss Brooks: I'm not able to give a Negro his manhood. Do you understand what I mean?"

"No, I can't."

"If you protect a dog against a hard master, do you give the dog manhood?"

"No."

"Precisely. So if you protect a Negro, as you would a dog, do you make the Negro a man?"

"I'm afraid I don't understand."

He patted her hand. "A prisoner needs too much to be able to understand, Miss Brooks, that protection can be less dignified than the lack of it."

And after the light midday meal the children had gone to their quarters, which had housed the garrison. They lived there with their mother, their uncle, the Morgan captain, and a Negro maid.

Colonel Trace and the silent one had gone riding, which she found they did every afternoon. Elvira and Howard were snugged into their original prison cottage. And the kitchen Negroes were silent or gone to wherever their quarters were. And Madi was alone in the prison, unless the captain was somewhere in the caverns below with his shovel.

She was alone except for the dog, which was nowhere to be seen, and the rats, which were nowhere to be seen. And Sarah? who was nowhere to be seen.

Madi thought she might take a nap.

She thought immediately that she might not. She felt a compulsive curiosity about the treadmill. Of all things in jail, she had found the treadmill the most humiliating. Yes, a guard ripping your dress was humiliating, but he might not rip it enough to make your flesh apparent to the curious. But the curious could and did see you on the treadmill, and there

51

was no way to hold things together, as was possible with a dress. You were on the mill, and you had to suffer it, and you could be watched, and people could witness the human being coming to her knees in supplication before her own basic fatigue, and no God, no strength, not even water, could deny them the opportunity of seeing you falter and become so much less than yourself that their cats at home on the cushions were better.

At least this treadmill here had been a useful force. The colonel had said that it was worn out, because the southern gentlemen had needed a great deal of bread. The treadmill she had been on had been as gratuitous a labor as the hand mill her mother had worked for ten thousand revolutions a day in the cell.

She was less afraid of the rotunda and the possible rats than she had been before because now it was the home where the rats lived. Naturally, she was no stranger to rats, but you hated to go into a new place and find a new tribe of them. Their ways might not be understandable, and, besides, you had to obtain the comfort of knowing that there they were and you had to get used to it. After a time they became a routine and your fright was as acute at a certain moment, but you recovered with a laugh and said to yourself, "Well, there they are again."

She thought that the workhouse would be at the far rear of the rotunda with its terraced cell block. Her acquaintance with this place had shown her that it was not at all like a jail. A jail was a workhouse surrounded by places for the prisoners to sleep. A place like this, where incarceration was the major procedure, not momentary detention, the work area was subordinate to the living quarters. Therefore the work area would be harbored at the back of the living cell block.

The stones of the rotunda floor were cut in oblong slabs that, if longer, would have seemed like cathedral crypts that she had seen in illustrations. But each slab here was roughly three or four feet long and about two feet wide, giving you the unsettling impression that if this was a crypt, it was one for children.

She couldn't tell whether the floor was echoing from caverns underneath or whether her steps beat against each far wall and the tiers of cells under the vaulted ceiling. But as she went across there was a booming sound that seemed to set her skirts adrift, as if sound itself was movement of wind. There was wind also, a firm, then unsteady flow of late, cold October, as if a drunken mill was unsteady. Her ankles, then her knees, then higher, prickled to this sea of floor, of silence, draft, and eyes that might be. She was brave because nothing showed itself except booming silence. A hollow, inflexible light, as if no day or night had ever existed, lived around her. Only if she looked upward could she see that there was a sky in this vast unpeopled room, and that the sky was a gray cave where you could suppose bats might hang, but she had never felt or seen erratic flight when darkness came.

There were a number of doors at the back, but she stopped in front of the one that was the most angry door. It was about five feet wide and about seven feet tall. The door to the temple, the kind of temple that people in here had to enter to make their kind of penitent prayer? Beside it was a staple in the wall. Next to the staple were two holes in the stone that might indicate where another staple had been.

Was this, then, the place where the example had been chained and exhibited so that others would not follow in his or her footsteps?

This seemed like the door that would be the one: ponderous, officious, massive, cruel with its staple.

She pulled on the gaunt ridged handle, which had crisp red edges that broke like dried blood into her hand. As the door opened, streams of afternoon light broke around the edge and cascaded on the floor. When the door was open far enough for her to look within, a soft voice said, "And you are Madelaine."

There was no doubt that this was the woman she had seen checking the graves. It wasn't only that there was no other woman here, it was that from the front this could not have been anything else but that woman.

Her intense back was bent in the same way, her patience was the same, her fiery hair was the same, and Madi could see that the same persistence, more powerful when looking at her face, was there and unalterable. Nothing could cut this woman down but the sword of time itself. It was there in the depth of the gaunt face, in the calm. She was animated stone, immutable. Madi was stunned. In the young eroded face there was a glacier. Implacable, running down a hillside, slowly, inexorably, with nothing that could stop it.

And in contrast her voice was a mere breath. As if you stood on a hill on a windless day and suddenly a portion of your hair was lifted by a wind and you looked up and around and tried to find it again, only to believe that it had not existed and you had been dreaming.

And contrast was not over: in comparison to the voice the mood and levity of the eyes was extraordinary. The eyes laughed. They had deep laughter. The eyes were young, as they must have been. The cheeks were drained of the cotillion, the young dance, love. The cheeks were gray-brown, from caverns. From the thought of them touching the cheeks? Only the eyes were what Madi conceived a southern belle to have been like, and she knew, at once, instinctively, that this woman had been one.

And only after experiencing the power of the face could she see the broken nails on the serene hands lying in the lap of the man pants. The hands that were digging for love for two years into earth no matter how deep.

In front of the eyes, the gauntness, the hands, and the intolerable patience, Madi felt awe and respect. Here was a woman of passion and iron.

"I'm Sarah Bruce Trace," said the woman.

"Sarah?"

The woman laughed. "Yes, Sarah. So you already know about the Sarah here? Well, I suppose I have a bigger appetite than she does. At this point, at any rate."

Mrs. Trace was sitting on a large wooden circular mill of some kind. It had ball bearings of wood all around its edge, and wooden spokes stuck out all around the edge. In the center of the circle, behind Mrs. Trace, was a metal cover with a rusted handle. To the right of Madi loomed the treadmill. It was not like the one she had known so well in the jail. That had been a level mill. This one was slanted at about a forty-five-degree angle and had iron horizontal flanges on which she assumed the men would climb so that the gears below would grind the grain. She assumed that the mill on which Mrs. Trace sat was for another part of the milling function.

But it was not the two mills that caught her real attention, and, once she had seen the power of Mrs. Trace, it was no longer the woman that held her. It was the great oval locket that hung from a chain around her neck.

At first Madi thought the convex surface of the locket contained a picture of Colonel Trace. But as she stared at it she realized that the locket held the portrait of the brother. Could they have been twins? No, the colonel was too young to be the father of the three girls.

"Your eyes are very blue when they open so wide," said

Mrs. Trace. She touched the portrait on the golden rim with one dirt-stained finger. "This makes you think of Colonel Trace, does it not?"

"Yes, ma'am."

Mrs. Trace's smile increased. Proudly she said, "It is Colonel Trace. But not such as Colonel Harte Trace"—she laughed, a soft, trilling, contemptuous laugh —"this is Colonel Jeb Trace my husband." And her finger made a definite passionate rhythm on the edge of the frame.

Madi could say nothing.

"Polly Ann told me that she got in bed with you the other night."

"Oh. Well, I didn't know whether I was dreaming."

"You weren't dreaming. She's a fierce, spiteful little wench. Sort of like her mother. There's some spite and fierceness running in the family, and she gets it from her daddy, and she gets it from me. She doesn't get the spite from her daddy, no, he was the leastest man of spite, barrin' none. He had no need for spite because there was nothin' he didn't have, and he would have kept it all if it wasn't for this place." She looked around, flame in her hair, light burning on the inertia of the treadmill and spilling over the mill on which she sat, and light edging the gold rim of the locket. Madi knew that in the locket would be strands of golden hair.

"Why, Polly Ann came to me and right proudly proclaimed her change of allegiance." The deep, soft smile was deeper and softer. "She told me you smelled a sight better than I ever could, at least in her recent memory. I smell of dirt and rats and worms. I supposed she wouldn't mind that if I wasn't so tired at the end of the day that my arms can't go around a child with any meaning. Come sit by me here, you don't have to stand there. Does Colonel Harte Trace keep you at attention?" There was mockery on his rank.

Madi sat beside her on the mill. It wasn't until she sat beside her that she realized Mrs. Trace was much larger than she had thought. Mrs. Trace was so well proportioned that her size did not reveal itself until there was a basis of comparison.

"I'm afraid I can't fight for the affection of my children——" began Mrs. Trace.

"I assure you——"

Mrs. Trace laughed. The soft laugh had a vibrancy that expanded its size in the room. "Don't worry yourself. You couldn't take my children away. They might just want to

bruise me, but fierce blood sometimes does. But it doesn'
mean anything. You don't separate blood like ours. No
usually. There're some Harte Traces in any world, even th
one we come from. But not many. That's why with no equip
ment and outmanned ten to one, the North could hardly bea
us. That's why." She paused and was passive a long momen
"So don't weary yourself thinking you're going to bother
family. You're not. They'll use you. They'll use the nigger
The niggers do the same thing, scratchin' around children t
better their lot, in their own minds anyway. It's a cold nigh
for a long time if all you can ever do is look in the window

"But if a barn was burning and all of us were asleep bu
the children, they'd drag me out, and my brother, Halsey
and the corpse of their daddy if we can find it. They migh
think of you-all later, if it didn't seem too late." She grinnec
"They might even think of *Colonel* Harte Trace. He might b
amusin' again someday." She put back her head and laughec
but the laughter stopped and she stared at the floor betwee
her boots.

She tamped the floor with her foot. "They're down there
all ten of them. It might sound disgraceful to you that I tal
this way, but you only need a look at Elvira to know ther
can't be any secrets. Her mouth is as full of things to let ou
as a boy catfish. A boy catfish goes around with his chillun i
his mouth driving him crazy and finally he spews them ou
He waits a decent time, at least, but Elvira wouldn't.

"But Halsey and me aren't disgraceful. No matter wha
Colonel Harte Trace might say or pretend to himself h
thinks. You don't neglect children by looking for their fathe
You neglect children if you don't find him!

"He must have a burial with honor. He isn't a bone lyin
somewhere in Yankee soil. He isn't fertilizer.

"Children are selfish when they're young. Mostly the onl
instincts they have are to suck something and have somebod
make play over them. But all the time in their minds the
know the important things. That's why I told you about th
burning barn. All the time they *really* know.

"And one day, after all they've had is some sugar to suc
on, they ask the question. Where's my daddy and wha
happened to him? Why did you leave him lyin' someplac
that wasn't his?

"Their daddy and their Uncle Halsey were with Morgan
and nobody was left behind, dead or alive. When you wer
with Morgan, you got home again.

"When you fell, two riders picked you up from each sid

and you got out of there. And if a man was left on the field, and the cavalry of Morgan had been driven from the field by cannon or overwhelmin' odds, they turned and charged!"

Reflectively, after a while, she said, "But even that way, you couldn't get everyone. They couldn't find Jeb. His horse was shot out from under him. He fell down into a ditch. His men fought all that night, making forays to try to find him. He was somewhere down there in the brush and stones. He couldn't be found. He wasn't found by the Yankees for a couple of days, some sentries scrambling down a bank found him, and finally he got here. And he's here still. He couldn't be anywhere else."

Her hair burned in the light. She was staring at the floor. "As I said before, it seems disgraceful to be here. It's a dishonor to the brother of my husband. But we've given Harte every benefit of the doubt. We've spent two years finding out that Jeb can lie nowhere else but under this floor."

Madi was very still.

Mrs. Trace said, "Say anything you want to say. I'm too tired and I've said too much to be the lady. I work in the fields. My hands tell you that."

Madi spoke carefully. "I've understood that Colonel Trace is very much against killing."

Mrs. Trace laughed under her breath. "He kissed you, is that what makes you so kind? Or didn't you know he did? Polly Ann got in bed with you. Polly Ann wouldn't go to sleep in bed with you; she'd want to have all the fun of knowing she was having vengeance on me, and you can't savor that properly if you're asleep. She saw that big fool Harte come in and kiss you. And she's told me her secrets. If the children seem a little sleepy sometimes, it's because they know the time when the *colonel* gets up the nerve to go up and kiss you again, and they wait in the cell next door and then slip out and look in when the damned romantic cowardly idiot is doing it again.

"No, Harte could never kill anyone. Not directly. No. Jeb could use the saber and the pistol. Harte never could." Her voice was softer than Madi had heard it so far. "Harte's the younger brother. Something seemed to have been left out of him. On the other hand, maybe something was put in. Something for another time, maybe. Not something that could be used in the agony of the South."

Her voice was soft. "It was a long time ago." A reminis-

57

cent smile was on her face. "Our plantation was only a few miles from theirs. Jeb was courting me. Harte was always following Jeb around, always. Jeb was pretty tolerant, but he could get pretty mad. This one day I was on the lower veranda and saw Jeb riding across the fields toward the lawns. Jeb never rode up the avenue. He was cavalry, even way back then, and it seems so long ago.

"I was looking over there, and Harte was trying to follow him. Between the fields and the lawn there was a stone fence and a ditch. The ditch was dry most of the time, but it was a part of a project my father had to make the fields more fertile. Our yield had been going down even some years before the war. Inefficient labor—the slave thing never was really good—and just not enough different kinds of crops. But we were happy. It seems like a dream since then. It seems as if a whole mist has gone down over it. It was a dream! But I know I lived in it." She paused. "Halsey knows. Halsey even knows where the dream came from. I never did, I never bothered. It was enough to dream it.

"I was looking over there," she said, the gauntness rounding out on her cheeks, "and Jeb was taking the stumps, the brush, the wall. Jeb rode like the devil himself. Or, to put it another way, when it came time to matter, Jeb, and the others like him, rode like the angels of deliverance. It's just that there weren't enough of them. Ten thousand more, that's all. Just ten thousand more, and it would all have been different.

"When Harte came to the wall, his horse must have felt the hesitation in the knees. The horse did not obey properly. It shied, and Harte was off on the ground. It wasn't the first time, no preacher. He had kissed the hem before.

"When Jeb came in the house, not even looking back, he went first to see my father. There was always a discussion and something to drink. I didn't stand there looking out at Harte. I sat down at the piano and began to play, very softly, so that when Harte came to the veranda, he would not think I had just begun to do so.

"He came in. He had put himself in well array, although you could see he had grassed.

"I didn't laugh. I allowed myself to play louder, but making it a gradual thing, so he could get used to it. I felt him standing behind my shoulder. Even then he was wearing his hair in the same way as his brother's, and some air came in and teased my face with it.

"It was the first time he ever told me one of his poems. I

58

don't know whether it is a bad or good poem. Perhaps you don't realize it, but the women of the South, ordinarily, were not well educated. We were educated in many ways—manners, grooming, music. And how to run a house from a decent distance, but we did not know prose or poetry except as it might inspire us. But that's the mostest of the things we knew. But I can remember his poem, more or less:

> "Fire, the first thing of man, reposes
> In your hair,
> That in times primordial
> Gave solace, to the spirit
> That could not then know God,
>   But God willing would."

Mrs. Trace stood up and walked from the room, her steps sounding booted over the rotunda, on the stone cavernous floor, and echoing from the ceiling, and silence. And Madi sat on the round golden-colored mill beside the treadmill with worn iron steps on which the young men had trod the hours for the grain that they would eat.

Madi remained sitting in the emotional trap that Mrs. Trace had developed for her. Mrs. Trace hated Colonel Harte Trace, but Mrs. Trace did not hate the colonel. Mrs. Trace believed, and, Madi felt, quite sincerely, that her husband's body was somewhere in this institution, and therefore his brother had killed him, and yet Mrs. Trace believed that her husband's brother was incapable of killing.

What solution could there be to all this? If any?

Was there actually the body, the skeleton perhaps, of a southern cavalry colonel somewhere down in the caverns of this place? Or were Mrs. Trace and her brother merely trying a last spiteful, fierce resort? After all, she had said that those were some of the characteristics of the family.

She felt a movement against her skirts, and then claws. She screamed and jumped up onto the cover of the mill. The mill began to roll on its wooden bearings. She shook the rat out of her clothing and it scurried into a hole somewhere in the cover and she sat on the metal inset beside the handle and shuddered from head to foot. She began to rub stockings, petticoat, and dress where the rat had been, and the wet was on her hand. The filthy thing had probably been in a sewer. A jerk of her mind pulled her head around and she expected to see something else disconcerting, but it was only Jenkins standing in the doorway, with his red-gouged-healed wounded neck and mute command. He pointed, and she knew she was to go to the colonel's office.

In the colonel's office the children were waiting. "They're going to take you up the mountain a way, Miss Brooks, to see the foliage."

That afternoon she tried to find hypocrisy in the children, that promised in the ultimate by Mrs. Trace; but she could not find it. They were outward, emotionally hungry, sweet, too-active children. Children everywhere, anywhere. Children.

Polly Ann, for example, who had slept with her, did not seem to have a mind filled with conspiracy, and the other two, whom Madi had thought would be jealous if Polly Ann had used force, did not seem to dissemble and were, as far as that goes, so fond of their sister that she had to get bored with them.

Madi got Polly Ann aside for a moment. "Polly Ann, be truthful, why did you come to sleep with me?"

Polly Ann's cheeks got red. "Madelaine, you seemed so afraid!" And she ran off to play with the others.

The few days had run off with her in a drama of personality that did not let her know where she stood, not only with anyone else but with herself. This morning she had confronted the colonel with the lack of materials and he had been embarrassed and had used Jenkins to reinforce himself. And she had felt pity for him; but the pity was like a mold of soft, to-be-hardened stone, into which metal bars are pushed. Her pity for him was soft, but her belief that there was something more was the iron bar.

She had gotten her analogy from another dinner with him. Tonight's.

"We've only used native materials so far in prison construction, Miss Brooks. Stone in mountain areas, brick in others. But I feel that the majority of construction henceforth will be of other materials. Sand and stone and iron or steel reinforcement.

"The more inactive a prison can become, the more the prisoner will be able to become a more constructive person. When I say inactive, I don't mean that they should do nothing or do meaningless tasks. I mean inactive in terms of dreaming of nothing except escape rather than reformation. Escape must be made impossible."

"I understand that you write poetry, sir."

He flushed. "As a gentleman officer, I have done many things. I have been active in operating a plantation, I have made my choice about freedom or nonfreedom for the slaves, and have fought in the cause, and I have been an incorruptible prison officer, once such an odious duty was imposed upon me. I have written poetry, yes. An exercise. I have done many exercises. I don't think that a fighting man must be insensitive."

"I don't either," said Madi. "If I may presume, could I have some of your poetry to read?"

"You can't presume anything, goddamnit. Now, you girls put your heads down where they were before and finish the fuc—, ah, stew."

The three girls glowed over their spoons with unlaughed laughter that might mean knowledge. Madi had heard the word and did not want to believe that the children had.

"How was the foliage this afternoon, Miss Brooks?" asked the colonel.

"Wonderful! But what is that pit up there, sir?"

"Pit?"

The silent man who had been serving them paused.

"The one that shines like an eye after it rains," said Marcy, the youngest.

"Shines like an eye!" repeated the colonel sarcastically. "Are you trying to be a poet too?"

"It shines like a blue eye," Marcy said fiercely, defending her envisionment of the pit.

"It shines like a mudhole," said the colonel.

"It would be nice to sail boats on," said Marcy. "It's sea-blue."

"Nonsense," said the colonel.

The silent man stood there.

"What the hell's wrong with you, Jenkins?" said the colonel. "I'll tell you what's wrong with you, Jenkins. I told you to have that pit fenced off. I suppose you did not think it was necessary. Now you know better. They went back there against my orders. What kind of soldiers are you girls? I'll tell you what kind. Insubordinate!"

"It wouldn't be practical to sail boats down there anyway," said Liz.

"All you ever say is practical," said Marcy. "You don't know anythin' else to say."

"I learned it from Auntie Close. She said it's practical for her to know she's a nigger, and it's practical for everybody

61

else to know the truth. And it's true you can't sail boats down there. Anyway, there's a brook."

"The brook isn't mysterious!" challenged Marcy.

"Who cares?" said Liz.

"The pit isn't mysterious," the colonel said gently to the little girl. "The pit is dangerous."

"That's what makes it mysterious," said Marcy.

Polly Ann was not joining in the conversation, and did not seem much interested in it. At mealtime Polly Ann was more deeply interested in food than the others, Madi had noticed.

"What kind of pit was it, sir?" asked Madi. "I could see that it isn't a natural pit but has been cut. Was it a quarry of some sort?"

"Originally, yes," said the colonel. "There are several of them around here, but that one, the one that fascinates Marcy, is the one closest to the . . . to the house. The rock face goes down fairly deep and was quarried, as were other stone faces, in order to build these buildings. Then it was discovered that the wells were inadequate for the large population here, and it was very expensive to dig wells deep enough to provide an ample supply of water. So that particular pit was used as the fountainhead, so to speak, for a cistern that supplied the installation with water. Since the war, no water having been drawn off, the amount of water entering the cisterns has eroded the walls, and they are now unusable, which is why we resort to the wells, one of them at any rate. And the supply is adequate for us."

"The sky shines into the bottom," said Marcy.

"I daresay it does," said the colonel. "It can't properly avoid it."

The silent man brought tarts. Marcy and Liz screamed with joy. Polly Ann looked at hers solemnly. Madi had the notion that Polly Ann's tart was more important to her than the tarts were to the other girls. She saw the girl's throat gulp. But Polly Ann had control; she ate her tart with decorum, while the other two wolfed theirs.

After Auntie Close had taken the children off to their quarters, after each child had first given Uncle Harte and then Madi a tart kiss, the colonel sighed and asked Madi if she would have a brandy with her coffee. She replied that she would like it very much indeed.

"I don't want to reprimand you," he said, "but I think it was improper for you to allow them, and yourself, to linger around a dangerous bit of terrain."

"We didn't linger, sir," she said. "As soon as I saw the pit, it frightened me. I was curious and we stayed a few moments, but the children were too skittish to linger there."

"Skittish?"

"Excited. You know how children are when they are showing you a secret?"

"A secret?"

"A forbidden, dangerous place is a secret in a child's mind."

"Of course it is," said the colonel, "of course. I think we found the right person in you to take care of them. You have the understanding."

He sniffed his brandy and held it to the light. "Do you know why the ancients called good things to drink *spirits*?"

"I'm afraid I don't."

"It was because they felt liquor was too good a thing for man to discover, and that it was a gift from the gods and made you a god when you drank it. The spirits of the gods were in the stuff."

As he talked, Madi could tell that he was thinking of something else.

"Even Noah got it from God," he said. "When the ark rested on Ararat, God had a present waiting for Noah. Grapes. They say that most of the vines for our best wines were taken from those that Noah found in the first light and safety after the flood." His prismed glass and liquor was turned in the light, then brought to nose and lips and a part of it drunk.

"An intelligence agent happened to be close when you and Sarah Bruce were talking," he said. "Jenkins patrols to see what's happening to the rat population, and he could not help overhearing the discussion.

"I understand that Sarah Bruce told you that I sneak about in the night and steal kisses?"

Madi flushed.

"This information," he went on, "has been confirmed by Polly Ann, who was sleeping with you the first time it happened. So intrigued was Polly Ann by this clandestine performance that she brought the other children in on it, and they have used it since as a form of entertainment."

"I——"

"I don't doubt that Polly Ann saw someone kiss you, or imagined she did—and if you thought that someone kissed you—Did you?"

"Yes," she said firmly.

"All right, then. Polly Ann saw someone kiss you, but it was dark and she was half-asleep, and she would naturally think it was me. She would do so because she is oriented to believe that I am a romantic."

"And aren't you?" she asked in a manner that surprised her. She did not want him to deny that he was a romantic. No matter what Elvira or Mrs. Trace or Halsey might think of him and his lack of blood lust, she appreciated his lack of blood lust. She had seen enough dirt with more in it than dirt to desire above anything on earth the glimmer of idealism and romance, even if, at a given time, a war, it could be considered incompetence or even cowardice. And she did not recoil from the fact that there had in conversations been implications that this man was a coward. She no longer believed there was the remotest possibility that he had killed his brother, and she did not think that anyone else thought so either. The most that could have happened was that Harte Trace, essentially not a soldier, no matter how romantically he inclined to be, had made another blunder, and his fierce soldier brother and cohorts had made or attempted an escape, and it had been thwarted by the watchful Jenkins, and Harte Trace knew no more about it than anyone else. Only that silent throat knew, and no one could make it speak, she was sure, even in handwriting.

"A romantic?" he said. "No, I'm not a romantic. To be passionate and write poetry isn't necessarily to be a romantic. To be a soldier and penal officer and be proud of the first, although hating to kill, and to be ashamed of the second is not to be a romantic. A romantic is someone who cannot see the immediate landscape because he doesn't want to. Because something in him will be destroyed if he does.

"There is romance in Polly Ann, romance and high spirits, high spirits it will be hard for you to find because she is like her mother and my brother and Halsey. She is the oldest of the girls, so she remembers the mist in which they all lived, the romantic mist out of which came some of the best soldiers ever to fight since the beginning of history. Under the flag of the Confederacy, they fought for a dream, a dream that never existed. They fought for a Southland that had never been. They fought for a gallantry that descended from a gallantry that had never happened, that was a myth in a brutal age where myths were necessary or men and women would believe in nothing and cut their own throats.

"Polly Ann would believe that I was the one who would be the figure in the dark that would bend over you and kiss you.

You yourself would believe that. Polly Ann is hungry and so are you. So you see what will feed your needs.

"But the children did not go up there to see me return, to their delight. You have never seen them sleep. They sleep like soldiers in the field after the day's battle. Like formless, mindless logs. Like the dead. And they are soldiers off a field each day, as uncertain as soldiers who have managed to exist for the day. They only vaguely know what is happening to them. I make sure of that, as contradictory as it seems. Because I am convinced they would be more frightened, more exaggerated in their emotions, than they are, if they truly knew everything.

"In ordinary times a man's emotions are shadings of all kinds, drifting simply from light to shadow, to half-light. You only know when a man is distraught, near the breaking point, when you see the absolute basis of his character in definable profile. In other words, an exaggeration of self.

"We have three little girls here. And even at such a simple time as supper, we have seen—I'm sure you saw it—three little girls who are exaggerated.

"Marcy is a dreamer, but she showed it too much. Liz is practical, but she showed it too much. Polly Ann is starving for the past, but she showed it too much. Not three little girls. Three definitions. Just as men in combat are of only one dimension. There is no room for them to be anything else but what is the foundation of themselves. They are more than that, all of them are more than that, but in uncertainty they can't be. There are reduced to the most prominent particle of themselves."

He sipped his coffee. "Anyway, as far as their watching is concerned, Auntie Close sleeps in the outer room, and her old ears hear a feather turning. They could not pass her."

He smiled as he looked at Madi. "Then, who kissed you? It was not me. I have indicated it would be good sport to kiss you and do more, for that matter. But you are in my charge and vulnerable to me. Therefore, unfortunately, I may not touch you.

"Did my brother kiss you? If the children actually managed to watch and you were kissed by me, or so they thought, then it would have been my brother, another ghost in the house. I think Sarah will suffice for ghosts."

"You don't believe in her?" She spoke haughtily because he was a self-confessed liar.

"In Sarah? Of course, I believe in the ghost of Sarah. I don't believe that she ran around aiding and abetting south-

65

ern gentlemen in finding exit from this place, and I don'
believe she'll rush to the aid of Halsey and Sarah Bruce i
their attempts to find bodies. But I believe she is here. I com
from an old world. Not old in point of time, but old i
tradition. You can't go now to an old plantation house i
Mississippi or Alabama without knowing as you walk throug
that invisible people are there.

"Passion, hurt, stays where it was. It doesn't go away
Something captures it and holds it there. Just like the exag
geration you can find in a person under certain circum
stances, that sharpness molds itself to walls and places. Yo
can go out into a countryside, and all of it will seem th
same, but when you come to the part of it that was a
battlefield, you'll feel the difference. I can tell you that. It'
much quieter there. And it isn't the imagination. There's no
so much wildlife there. A battlefield is hushed, and all aroun
it are the sounds of bright living life."

His green eyes were deeper, his golden hair swept bac
over his shoulders. The fire and the lamps were static wit
light. As she listened she heard his voice return to its origina
idiom.

"Why, I remember the first time I knew that. As vivid a
the light on the glass. I was almost thirteen, a thrivin' bra
but a sadness here and there. I took some little meat and a
piece of bread and went off, outside Natchez. Our mothe
tol' us never to go there. It was a pretty day. Everythin' wa
sort of moving around and dancing, callin' to you: 'I'm a
pretty girl today.' Days are like that.

"I sat under the live oaks, happy as you please. I ate an
whistled, but I remember I didn't do it much. Everythin' wa
polished. Leaves and branches were like handles on some
thing. I knew why I was there.

"I walked around and stood rooted to a spot. I felt fire o
the bottom of my shoes. Not the kind that could destroy m
or even really burn. It came up my legs to my heart and hel
me there, and I looked down and that patch of grass was a
circle greener than any grass I had ever seen. I stood ther
and a few tears came out, but they were hard. It felt lik
round pieces of glass, a little rough on the edges, wer
comin' out and sliding off my face without hardly touchin
the face at all."

He smiled reminiscently.

"I went back and got Uncle Henry. He always liked m
and he knew our history, down to the finest dot. We got bac
there, and I said, 'Uncle Henry, where did my father die?'

"Without any hesitation, he walked to the spot where I had been standin'. Uncle Henry had been my father's second that day, and he knew just where he had fallen."

He picked up his brandy glass and turned it in the light.

"Our family was brought up in the code duello. Not in the French way. English. But down in Mississippi and Louisiana we call it the code duello, just as the Spanish and French did. And still do, if the truth be known.

"You've probably been wondering why I've been following these people around for the past two years, if it wasn't for the fact that I'm afraid they're going to find something, and if I can find it first, I can cover it up again.

"That isn't the reason. Halsey told me I killed his sister's husband. I slapped him in the face. He challenged me. I had to accept. I left the tradition, and I fought the South, but I was brought up in such a way I can't refuse a challenge.

"But Halsey's a gentleman. He's giving me a chance. If they can't find Jeb, or what they think is Jeb, then we don't fight. If they find him, we fight.

"They've done everything they could to prove me inno-cent, I'll have to say that. They've dug every grave from here to Natchez.

"They've found a lot of them, not Jeb and the other nine, but a lot of the others from other prisons that never got home. It was a trail of horror from prisons up here back to the South. If they got to starving too much and stole, and were caught, they were hung. If they begged, the farmer would say they should wait a minute and he'd come back and blow their heads off with a shotgun and then he was a hero. There were times when some of them holed up in a barn and the community set the barn afire. If anybody shot one of them down when he ran out, that anybody got a prize. They took a boy and put him on a pole and it took him twenty four hours . . ."

The colonel's voice trailed off. The light shone between them. Madi had forgotten her brandy, but remembered and drank it. The brandy shone in her belly.

The colonel's voice had shown signs of a tremble. It firmed off. "Halsey, the man of tunnels, the one who wants to find some bones, any bones, and kill me in a duel is the one who is kissing you. Who else could it be? A jail cell can't be locked from the inside, but Jenkins could lock you in every night."

She shuddered. "No, thank you."

"Maybe it's been Jenkins that's been kissing you."

Jenkins wasn't there, so she allowed herself to wince.

Colonel Trace said, "Howard would be too afraid of Elvira to chance it."

"Why would the Captain kiss me?"

"His mind has some crevices——"

"It takes that to kiss me?"

"I wouldn't say so, but it would take it in him."

"Because he was with Morgan, and Morgan defeated you?"

"I'm glad to see—or to hear is better—that you feel at home enough not to be afraid to be a bitch. Morgan didn't defeat me. I told you I'm a liar. I'm not. The reason I told you that was because I had spent a good part of a day listening to Halsey and Sarah Bruce telling me I was a liar. I hadn't said a good goddamn word to them the whole day except what was elicited. But they chose to call me a liar, because the whole South wanted back then in the war to make-believe that I hadn't beaten Morgan."

He was such a liar that it was unbearable. Was it the brandy, was it herself, was it both? Madly she stood up and said, "Everyone knows you can't hurt anything, so how could you win a war?"

It was so fast that there was no breath in her after finishing what she had said. He was around the table and his fingers feeling long and powerful were squeezing her neck and pressing her head back, and she did not even have the breath she could have drawn after speaking if he had not come so fast.

He's killing me, she thought.

Black drowning. A small point of golden light, beacon in dark was the last place she saw.

When a flexible whirl, slight and distant, began to sway in front of her, she knew how far away she had been, and was aware that she had been in a very dark place where nothing existed. It was the first time that she had been in such a place; sleep certainly did not provide it. Sleep, no matter how abrupt if you were dreadfully tired, did not engender this terror of having been in a pit, one so long and black that it was as nonexistent as you were. Even as she was emerging from it she doubted her mother's thoughts about the afterlife. There was nothing down there. It was dark and endless.

She did not know where she had been a few moments before. Memory that was attached to the beginning of her consciousness did not include the most recent happenings. It

ncluded fragments of the past and present, and when her eyes
opened, she was surprised to see the colonel sitting beside
her. So disoriented was she that she smiled to see him, as if it
were a happy event. After a moment she realized that she
must be lying on the dark brown leather seat of the long
wooden bench that was against the rear wall of the room. A
glow from the fire made wedges on the ceiling. She was
bemused by them, and her smile deepened. But a formless
ense of trouble was welling up in her and joined the form-
ess thoughts and images, and in her throat there was a sharp
burning sensation. When she tried to talk, her throat rasped
nd her tongue was hazy and rough.

"Har . . ."

"Don't try to talk," he said.

He was leaning over her, and his curls were against the
side of her cheek, as they had been the first time, when he
had come to her room to greet her, and she had had the
ensation that he was going to kiss her.

His face loomed, and the emerald eyes were lighted and she
saw his dry, lean mouth and tilted up to him and his
mouth settled on hers, gentle and pressing and moving, and
he moved her mouth on his, with an odd wish to make his
mouth wet, and she could feel it happening, and their mouths
were joined and wet.

She had the impression that she was giving him something
important, moistening the erosion of himself, and she drew
him to her with her mouth. She was shocked to know that
he could do this, for she had never done it before. Her neck
burned and ached, and the neck-fire seeped into her skull and
began to drift around like a fire in a wind burning white
wood. It hurt a very great deal. She wondered why the hurting
did not infuriate her and make her beat him. She was at the
doorway of a mystery of woman, which she had suspected
but never really known.

It was twice-over a mystery. She did not merely forgive
him, she did not believe that the man who had strangled her
was the same man who was solacing her. It was not that she
was deluded, or even that she wished to be. It was simply that
she could tell it was not the same man. The other man
existed, yes, he was real, he was no fantasm. But he was not
here now. The truth now was the man who had rescued her.
It did not matter that the two men were the same man—
what mattered was that she was rescued and being held
tenderly, and she was grateful. After all, the man she held in
her arms had been sorely tried and beaten by that other man,

69

too, just as she had been, and now they could solace each other and lie still (fairly still?) with each other.

But she had known, even as she had been experiencing her knowledge of woman and wounded man, that stillness was not going to be the issue. He was not coming a child to her breast, nor Antaeus to his mother, to spring strong again for combat. A man was aroused by her mouth and her posture.

She forgot her pain in anticipation of another that was only myth to her. She was fighting him again, but it was not the kind of fight she would have put up if she had known that he intended to strangle her. Nor did he use his quickness and power. They were opponents, but opponents with no real desire to injure each other.

She allowed his sweet aggression, he accepted the gentle repulse. But he would not let her get away, and, in truth, she could not get away. Only he could leave. She was the besieged village or castle, and that does not run. He was the cavalry and very resourceful in attempting to find her weak points and come upon them unexpectedly, pushing aside the local resistance.

It was warm and the firelight leaping, and she had wondered about this game. It was not until now that she realized that she had wondered about it quite often. She hadn't remembered until now that she had sometimes lain in bed and wondered how it was played. Many reasons had made her choose not to remember: in the jail, with her mother lying sick beside her, she had thought about it. And it had been like this somewhat, although of course not so detailed, because the details had been unknown to her. She had been ashamed to dream so when her mother was ill—but lying under the ceiling that danced with reflection, she wondered whether her mother had dreamed also. This had happened to her, and she could remember. Was that why she had lain so quiet, with her breathing softer? That she remembered?

She heard herself commanding, and Harte Trace, Colonel Harte Trace, was pleading.

Power.

It filled her lungs with air. It expanded her, it made her even stronger. And even as his attempts became stronger, she was stronger still, and he did not dare cross her boundaries.

Power.

She would torment him!

Even as she refused she accepted. Even as she turned him

70

away she kissed him; and when he came back, she humiliated him with hauteur.

She was dizzy with fascination. She could do anything with him that she wanted to. He was helpless.

She bit his ear at the same time as she pushed his hand angrily. She murmured into his breathing at the same time as she turned her hips.

Intoxication. She could do this? He was broken.

Everything fled away. She was Madelaine Brooks, mistress of the manor. And in her decision, in her imperial hand, all things were possible. Or impossible.

It was wild, delicious. A ringing gypsy song.

You will not do that. That is not permitted. Do you wish to make me angry? You have some things to answer for already. I will kiss you if you don't get wild. Don't you think you are making yourself suffer? If I give you that privilege, will you contain yourself? Well, your promises have not been very good so far, I must say.

There was no other world and there never had been. It was all gone now. And it was not the world of the darkness to which she had been subjected—by him—but her return was to him, and this was a world of surrounding dark and light and warmth here, and contest in which she was the master. As she had never been before.

It was more important than any world she could have imagined. He could have easily raped her, but that was not good enough for him. He had given her command so that what he got, if he did, would have value.

Even so, he was raping her. He could not help doing some of it. His mouth was raping her, and his tongue made the attempt. When she bit his tongue and some blood flowed into her mouth, she felt herself move convulsively against him. This was the first vibrant substance exchanged between her and someone else.

A part of the life of someone else had been drunk by her mouth.

No brandy could burst in her that way, and she had to stop herself from sucking his wound, in a yearning hunger to absorb more of him.

She came to a stage past delight. Revenge. Vengeance. He had hurt her. But he was not the only one who had done so. She could put him on a treadmill. With a few motions and a few rejections, she could make her chained prisoner moan more than anyone she had heard. She was his jail and she was a better jail than any that could be built of other materials. No jail that man could ever devise could hold a prisoner the way she could hold him, and make him eager for more of his torment, not to escape from it. She did not need iron and stone. All she needed was a light flutter of her fingers on his back, and he could not go anywhere.

She had suffered, and he must pay the price. She wished to tell him so. "I want to hurt you," she said. "I'm going to scratch you." She drew her nails along his cheek. She did not do it lightly; this was no token. She intended to draw blood, and she did. And he kissed the fingers that had drawn the blood.

"I had to kneel to come here to you," she said. "Now it's your turn."

He knelt beside the bench and took off her boot and kissed her toes through her stockings.

When he got beside her again and kissed her mouth, she remembered that she had forgotten to change her stockings that morning.

It didn't matter to him—he was far beyond that point—so she decided that it did not matter to her. Anyway, how could it? By this time they both were such a mass of rumpled clothing in distress that she wondered about parts of the world where these things were conducted in a less complicated fashion, at least as far as clothes were concerned.

However, there was something to be said for the mess. If you had difficulty finding something, it gained in value. Who would want gold if you could pick it up like pebbles?

She laughed; she was in another stage. She did not want revenge anymore, she had had that. Now she was worldly and wise and conducting a salon into which ardent colonels were no exception.

She grasped his head and her fingers and nails raked through the golden curls. She took handfuls of them and pulled them and put hunks of them into her mouth and pulled on them. This is what she had wanted to do, wasn't it? And now she was doing it. Nothing could stop her now. She felt the beginning of the arch in her back. Hurt me, hurt me. You hurt me, but hurt me the real way.

There had been massive fires, from the bursting one of being strangled, to the brush fire of tenderness, to the small and enlarging flames of contest—so that fire was her soul, and no other, and only he could quench it. He could throw fury and appeasement against and into her, and burn against

72

her fires and flash them out as they screamed, and would they scream? She wanted to scream.

Endearments.

The fire on the ceiling and she turned back her head to watch and to be captured. I am your village, your house, conquered. Her door was undefended.

Her joy welled from her eyes and she clung to him with passionate tenderness for all the treasures he had given her: he had given her beauty because he wanted her, he had given her mastery and therefore dignity, he had given her power, he had given her revenge, he had given her the chance for fulfillment. Her world was full, and now it only remained for him to fill her again and break against her, thrusting every gift deep within her with another expected fire of pain and strength and release. Her arms were around him and the flood of her happy, hot, passionate tears cascaded down his neck.

The room went cold.

As soon as she knew it was not going to happen, she had closed her eyes, and when the wall of his body was apart from hers, the fire did not matter, the drafts from the walls crossed over her and the parts exposed.

"I'm sorry," he said formally.

She opened her eyes and saw him standing beside the bench above her. He had straightened himself out very well, very quickly. She supposed soldiers had that ability. If you couldn't get dressed quickly, you could get out of the bombardment only in your underwear.

She couldn't help but notice that what had been trying to ram her from all sides was no longer attempting to stretch his trousers.

She did not try to gather her clothes around her. She looked like a slut who had asked too large a price, so she was going to lie there that way.

The thing that hurt the most was that some of the hot tears had not learned their lesson as yet and still felt they were needed and were running down her face. The tears of gratitude that would have changed to the tears of injury that would have made her laugh and kick (she knew she would have kicked, she had been sure of it) and whisper something, she wondered what, in his ear.

"I'm sorry," he said, "I was carried away. But when you started to cry— If you'll forgive me? As I told you, I won't take anyone who is in my charge and vulnerable to me. Do you want me to escort you to your room?"

"No," she said. "You are a very gallant officer. I was disturbed that you were taking advantage of me, but I am helpless. I admire you for your courage in this case."

"May I help you?" he said.

"No!"

She began to labor up from the bench. Why did people wear so many damned clothes? Yes, she knew the word. And why were they so important, so that you had to kneel in a jail to get some?

She didn't know whether he went upstairs with her to her door. It didn't matter. The stairs felt laborious. Women she had talked to in the workhouse had told her that after you had walked the treadmill awhile your knees were never the same again.

She was glad to close the iron cell door around herself. "Hello, Sarah," she said to the somewhere nail marks on the wall. "At least I put mine into some skin."

You fool, Harte, you fool, you fool!

Didn't men know when you were ready?

⚘⟨ CHAPTER III ⟩⚘

MADI HAD LEARNED THAT A WOMAN, like the year itself, had seasons, but they were not animal seasons and were not regular, like those of the year: they were psychological and capricious, but they blew hot or cold. And in between. Thus it was by pure coincidence that as the weather grew colder into November she grew colder to Harte Trace.

The unfortunate thing was that she wished to forgive him; if it hadn't been for the important drive to forgive him, she wouldn't have so vividly remembered that he had insulted her. It did her no good whatever to know that his intent had not been at all insulting, but rather otherwise. Her intellect could not help her in the impasse. Her mind told her clearly that he had been trying to be a gentleman. But her emotions were stronger and less forgiving than her mind. Her emotions told her that she had been willing, and that he made her willing and then he had abandoned her. He had stepped away from her and quickly straightened himself, giving him the opportunity to look down at her dishevelment. But that had not been the least of the injuries. The most important loss she had sustained was the loss of the power she had held over him. She could not have retained that power, she instinctively knew, once he had possessed her, but she would have gained something in its place. His gratitude. She would have paid him back for her own.

Instead of all this, he came out of the field alone and the victor. He had vanquished her with embarrassment and he had emerged a martyr to his repression, sacrifice, and decent honor. Consequently, he had left her with the sour impulse that had been expected of her on more occasions than one—the Christian desire to wash his feet. And she hadn't wanted that. She had wanted to hold him in her arms while he briefly died of fatigue and she stroked his hair with sympathy and generosity.

He had robbed her without mercy, and no knowledge that it had not been that way at all could change her attitude.

The birches were white splayed fingers among the evergreens, and November was stiff on the ground. Elvira said, "The maniacs and the soldiers didn't die in November, ain't that strange? They died in October, when they knew winter was coming, and they died in December, I suppose when they knew Christmas was coming and it wasn't going to do them any good. In January they sort of froze up, the soldiers mainly. The maniacs didn't mind the cold half so much. A lot of cold weather must be in the head.

"It was strange though. In the spring the maniacs used to go out of their minds. The way animals do when they're caught up. Cats climbing up on anything, scratching to get out. The maniacs used to act like cats and howl like hunting dogs that are railed in in barns. You never heard the like.

"But the soldiers was just the opposite in the spring. Cheerful, getting as much of the light on themselves as they could. I guess they were hopeful, knowing the ground was getting soft and they could dig. You used to see them all the time, picking up dirt and feeling it as if it was gold. Yay-es, just as if it was real gold."

November was a mold around Madi also, affecting her in its own way for her purposes, or for her immediate reactions. It was a cold November. Howard told her that this year the frost line was going to be lower than it had ever been in most of the years of his life. He said that the frost line was supposed to be approximately the same every year, no matter what the temperature, but he said he knew better. If you had a vegetable cellar and a potato grew a green sprout, then the frost was going to sink far deeper into the ground than usual.

What Madi wanted for herself was the thing the soldiers had not wanted and that had depressed and killed some of them. She wanted the digging to stop.

She did not want Colonel Jeb Trace to be found this season.

She assumed that her conscience disturbed her because she was selfish. Assuming that her conscience bothered her was sufficient and then she did not have to think about it anymore. She was free to think about her selfishness.

Her life here was the best she had ever had. There had been no subtlety in the way that she had become a central figure in a power struggle. The power struggle did not have

76

well-formed lines: she was not precisely expected to win the children over to Harte Trace or to Mrs. Trace and her brother. She was expected, curiously, to keep the children neutral. Neutral, she gathered, was normal. Harte Trace believed the children should know nothing, and he treated them in a game-playing way. Mrs. Trace, also, did not believe in telling them what the quest was, but she believed in their knowing that it was serious and portentous, and took precedence over them and their present lives.

It was Madi's task to keep the children from hopeless confusion.

The children were hopelessly confused from two sides, therefore Madi's middle position was the most important oasis in their lives. It was an oasis that she attempted to keep as restful and sweet as possible, despite her feelings toward Harte. But the calm confidence they expected of her and that she, in her job, expected of herself was not always possible. It was not that she would verbally take one side or the other, it was that the children could tell whenever a particular wind was blowing through her ears. They did not want her to be unsure of anything. They wanted her to be a brick wall about four feet thick, and she had portions of her that were emotional tissue paper.

Her realization of this made her stern as a facade. This seemed helpful, rather than otherwise. Sternness might not be a brick wall, but it can resemble one, particularly if the need is present. On the one hand, Harte Trace was indulgent, and on the other, their mother was neglectfully indulgent. Both were quicksand. Madi was the word and the voice, and the stout platform on which indulgence was a reward, not a nebulous right based on mystery and enigmatic opposing forces.

Madi was the children's house; there were too many restless winds blowing through the others to be cozy.

It was good to have a ring of dependency around her, the three pairs of light gray eyes waiting for her to reveal, command, or demand. Madi herself had a history of dependency, of blankets on floors in the blurred houses and apartments of friends and relatives. Dependency on men and women who came to the flat and gave her and her mother attached strings of garments to sew. The gnawing looking-out of the window to see when father would come home with all he had promised. There had not seemed to be any end to it. What end was possible but the workhouse? She remembered her and her mother's hands trembling as they had assumed father's debts.

A man had put a stubby finger into the hollow of her shoulder.

"You are old enough to sign, young lady?"

"Yes, sir."

She had been doing something for this man, assuming a debt for which she was not truly responsible, and yet she had been afraid of him and grateful for the way he smiled at her when he picked up her signature and carried it away with him.

But there had always been something else. In the early morning clatter of horses' hooves on cobbles, her eyes had opened with a feeling of nails driven through the pupils, but she could still see. She could not only see outside, she could see inside. She had known that she was walking the course she was walking because it was her mother's wish. She had known that her mother for reasons she would keep to herself through all eternity was trying to pick up and clean the manhood her husband had left trailing on the ground behind him.

She was resentful that her mother would expect her to, also, would quietly accept her own dedication to this wild inexplicable cause—but just as father had probably been the only thing in mother's life, so mother was the only thing in hers. If there was only one thing, then you had to make it shine as well as possible, didn't you?

It wasn't only a levy on the lives of the children that made her life right now. She had a levy on the life of Harte Trace. As iron had sunk from the wind and the sky into the soil, Halsey had had to come up from his tunnels. He proved competitive.

He had smelled like a snake when Madi had first met him, when Sarah Bruce had invited her to their quarters to meet him.

Madi had stood before Harte's desk and said, "I wonder if I may have dinner with Mrs. Trace and Captain Selby? I've been invited."

"We don't call Captain Selby a captain anymore, if you don't mind? There is no Confederate army, and even if there was, he wouldn't be a captain because he has no military affiliation, nor is he retired. And in retirement we don't refer to captains in any case. I might add that Captain Selby was never a captain in a regular army sense. He had enough money to recruit some riders and he made himself a captain.

"It's extraordinary that they would invite a stranger but have not since we've been here invited the children?"

She flashed: "Perhaps they feel that because of the way you act, as if you're still commandant of this place, they'd have to ask your permission to invite the children?"

"It is not your prerogative to stand there and say those things, but I'll inform you that in strictest terms I still am the commandant of this place. I bought it. And it might also please you to know that they would damn well have to ask my permission to invite the children, because they are paupers and all expenses for this farce are paid by me.

"Their plantations are burned to the ground. Their gold supply of Negroes is sucking off of them or have wandered away.

"The money that goes out here to help them find my brother, so that Halsey can take his fucking dueling pistols and try to kill me, comes from me. Go have dinner with them, it's the same price as I'd have to pay to feed you here."

Her cheeks drew out blood. It was as if her outer skin pulled blood from inside her and flung it out into the room into a red haze before her eyes. And then the pinched vessels expanded and new blood filled them until the blood was storming her eyes and making her blind.

Not even in the workhouse had a man used a word like that before her. Not even a guard who would contemptuously touch her would say a word like that.

"I am not a barracks wench, Colonel. I would like your apology."

He stood up, pallid. "Forgive me, if you will. I was carried away. But I submit that is no excuse."

"You seem to remember the barracks very well."

"Yes," he said sadly, "I remember the barracks very well."

Madi picked her way over the stones of the yard, guiding herself by the light from the windows of the garrison cottage at the western end of the walled yard. It was a two-story building and there were four lights in windows on the downstairs section and two above. The light that comes after initial darkness in the cold months had not yet begun, but she could see smoke spiraling upward toward the deep sky.

The door was square, made of upright shaved planks, and there was a square of light around it. When she knocked, the door stood tight but a latch rattled. Mrs. Trace opened the door and the firelight from behind her swept across the indentation of one turned cheek and struck Madi with warmth. "Come in," she said.

As soon as Madi had walked inside she had forgotten the notion of poverty that Harte had provided for her. If poverty was here, it was not of the kind she had known.

It was true that the rugs on the floor were thin, but they seemed to her to be the kind that would be all right in a southern part of the country. She knew very little about rugs, but these could not be cheap. They had some of the dim brown-red-gray quality of tapestry. Springing light from the fire was a highboy with decanters on it and bright liquor in them. The chairs were old, deep, and comfortable. These were possessions that had been transported from a distance. She knew also that Mrs. Trace and her brother had riding horses. Would Harte Trace provide all this in order to further their search and stand him for a duel? Or would he do this to prove his innocence? Or was it defiance? And would these people accept it from him?

Sarah Bruce might. She had shown a sentimental past attachment to Harte Trace. But what about Captain Halsey Selby?

Halsey got up and came toward her, smiling. She had been shocked when she woke up her first day here and had seen Colonel Trace with his long golden curls and emerald eyes bending over her, but she was more shocked this time.

When she had first seen him, riding about the inner wall area of the prison, on the fine chestnut horse, waving saber and flag and wearing a Confederate uniform, yelling, she had noticed that he was not a large man. And she had thought that he was probably theatrical or crazy. And what Harte Trace had said about him had confirmed her opinion. That she had not seen him in all this time since, even making a performance on his horse, had further made her think he was very odd. Elvira had said, "He's got dirt on his mind. Maybe he thinks he's a gold or coal miner. It's only dirt. He's down there, down in the caverns, day and night. Day and night. And he believes in Sarah. Not his sister. Sarah the ghost. He believes she led them out, and then somebody stopped it. Guess who? Yay-es!"

"Good evenin'," said Halsey Selby. "Now I do believe,

within my discretion concerning gossip, that I've heard of you."

"It probably couldn't be avoided," said Madi.

"I'll get the dirt out of my ears," he said, "and then I'll be more glad of gossip."

He was holding her hand. She had put out her hand and he had taken it and he was lightly holding it.

He was beautifully dressed, but he smelled like a snake. He was wearing a thigh coat, old but made of a material that she did not recognize. The coat came to midthigh and was open over a tight golden vest. His trousers were gray and held over his black boots with dark, thin straps. His hair had red hues with silver and was worn to the nape. There it turned up in curls, on which the firelight showed the soft russet and the silver hue.

He was not large. His eyes reached to hers. His eyes were so calm they were almost an affront. He had no conclusions, he had no fears, he did not care what she thought of him. His eyes indicated that he was satisfied with himself and was not afraid.

How did she know that? Was it because of all her past experience? She supposed that it was. She had learned to read eyes, in the area of exposure to unpleasant experience, to anxiety, to fear. She even had known how to read her own, without bothering to look in the mirror. She had known what her eyes were like in a given circumstance.

His eyes were tawny and serene. He was well-dressed, but the smell of earth was around him, emanating from his pores. It was not simple to wash fully around here in this weather, and the fire was hot, making smells develop themselves. She was already making excuses for him.

It seemed a worthwhile enterprise. She looked at him and did not wish him to smell. And if he did, it was because of an intense underground adventure that was in the province of what a fierce man would do. His hand and eyes were so gentle that she knew from his smile that she had met the fiercest man of her life.

What do you think of this, Harte Trace?

"Your eyes are very direct," Halsey said.

"If you'll forgive me?"

"There's no need to," he said. "If you've listened to enough people around here, you are convinced my gunpowder blew up in my head." He laughed, his eyes crinkling long and thin with gentle amusement. There was no bluster about him.

81

There was an infinite, self-derogatory humor, as if he would disclaim any pretensions that anyone would offer him.

"And what are you doing with gunpowder at this point?" she asked, embarrassed because he had not dropped her hand.

"Trying not to blow up myself," he said. "Tryin' not to blow up the whole place. It makes a trying day. I'm a horseman, not an expert on blowing up things, but I have to do it. There are spaces down below there that it would take you a hundred years to try to get through if you didn't use somethin' to help."

"Gunpowder?" she asked, astonished.

"I call everything gunpowder," he said, "that blows up in such a way that it's gratifying."

He let go of her hand. He did not drop it; he made sure that it was poised on air and that she knew of his intention, and then he softly withdrew his hand.

"I've never heard anything," she said.

"You wouldn't be likely to," he said. "You certainly would be surprised to find how deep this place goes. And then, I use small charges and put mats over the place I'm exploding. It sounds right harsh down there, but I'd be surprised if you'd hear it up here."

"Sherry?" asked Mrs. Trace.

The three of them were still standing, and Madi took her fluted glass. It turned in her fingers as she accepted it, and firelight burst through the pale liquid and the prism of the glass tossed the light around her fingernails, making them glisten.

"Let's sit down," said Mrs. Trace. As soon as Madi sat down on the hearth sofa next to Halsey she realized that the furniture was older, or more worn, than she had thought. Somewhat less comfortable. She had been in more uncomfortable circumstances, but not in such a formal atmosphere. She wondered how long she should decently wait before shifting herself from a reinforcement that was more importunate than the fingers of any guard.

"We should have had another talk before this," Mrs. Trace said. "I surely know what you must think of me. If I neglect you, I neglect my children. I get letters all the time from friends and relatives, telling me I'm obsessed, and let the dead lie. But do you think they ever do?"

Madi was not ready with an interesting answer. She had an interesting problem on her hands, or, rather, beneath her. She could not sit here and be intelligent and listen and reply unless she managed to get off of whatever was sticking into her. It was a problem in manners. She was quite close to her edge of the sofa, and if she lifted herself and moved further to her own side, it might indicate that she was too well aware of how much Halsey smelled of newly turned earth. He did smell like what she imagined a gravedigger would smell like over his evening soup, but she did not want Halsey to realize that. She was a guest, therefore a courteous captive of whatever smell he happened to be wearing.

On the other hand, how could she be so forward as to lift herself (and she would have to lift herself; you couldn't slide off of this thing without some risk) and sit closer to him? It would indicate something she did not want to indicate, and it would be disloyal to her employer, no matter what a fool he was, and make Halsey and Mrs. Trace think she was snugging into their camp, which she had no intention of doing.

She wasn't going to snug into any camp.

What effrontery she had, deciding she didn't need to. Alms please? She would have none of that anymore, unless someone threw her out, charity trunk and all, and she found a treadmill waiting for her somewhere.

When whatever it was began to sink through fabric, she made her decision. It was in favor of not insulting Halsey.

"I'm awfully happy you invited me for another talk!" she exclaimed, lifting herself and planking herself down next to Halsey and touching his sleeve. "I wonder, sir, if you have any suggestions about the best way to handle the children? After all, I have not spoken to you before, and I so much want to do the best I can!"

She smiled and took her hand from his sleeve. Tilted her head in question, to hear his reply.

Mrs. Trace said, "You got off that dowel very neatly, my dear."

They all three threw their heads down in laughter.

Sarah Bruce Trace turned her glass, watching light attack the color and make an invasion and break off from it, returning to its source and coming back. She kept revolving her glass for a moment, with the attack and counterattack of light, and held the glass still, allowing the elements of light to make the glass of sherry a light amber. She looked down into the pure light in her glass, as into a depth where something was known. In the shallow depth she seemed to want to read, as if the illusion of depth took her far down below, to the places where Halsey had found dark, secret earth whose character he brought from a sunless pasture into upper air and light in his pores. He smelled of earth as if he had eaten of it as he would a strong spice and was sweating it into the room through clothes and skin.

"I'll tell you the truth," said Sarah Bruce at length. "I learned it at my daddy's knee. I used to like to sit on my daddy's knees. They aren't around anymore, some Yankee pirates came in one morning and shot his knees off and the rest of him. The deserters. We called them pirates, and they sailed over the countryside on horseflesh they stole from us.

"We buried Daddy in the grave he had dug before, where he buried the family plate. We put him on top of it and he protected it. When Yankees came around digging anyplace they could see that somebody had buried something, they found Daddy and left it that way, and we covered him up again. He protected what we had left better than if he had been standing up there with a pistol."

Sarah Bruce was talking about the family plate and the fires on the plantation and the one renegade Negro that they had had to hang, and how the man's wife had clung to Sarah Bruce, but of course nothing could be done, and she had talked on about the grave and when the war ended, they had taken Sarah Bruce's father from his temporary burial as ceremonial guardian of the fortune left and had buried him on top of the hill, his favorite spot, where the house in which he had been born had once stood.

None of this was lost on Madi, nor the firelight, nor the proximity of Halsey's thigh, nor the nostalgia in Sarah Bruce's voice. There was nothing that Sarah Bruce said that Madi agreed with. You did not execute the renegade Negro; he had the illusion he was free and could assert and rebel, just as she was doing in her own way. Were not these people compulsively seeking the very same kind of person, a man who would rebel and seek freedom, even if his brother was commandant of the prison and could be in difficulties because of a successful escape?

And yet as Sarah Bruce spoke, Madi understood. Sarah Bruce was talking about a kind of life that was a romance, an almost impossible dream, a world that Madi herself would have liked to have been in.

"The creek was near the big plantation house," said Sarah Bruce, "and the niggers would go down there walking soft in bare feet, gray on the sides and on the bottoms when you saw them lift their feet. There was sunshine all around and you'd sit on the veranda, either the one downstairs or up-stairs, and wave and smile. They were so happy. The women would carry the baskets on their heads and even moving their heads laughing and bowing, they would never topple one down. The rice boats had sails that were yellow and red. Flatboats, comin' up from the river. We had a mill with big, curved metal teeth, like a panther's. After the rice boats went off downriver, we'd flood the fields, just before autumn. The men were all excited, waiting for the birds and the deer. The birds were first, letting down when the dikes had been pulled up. After that it was tundra, and sometimes there was morn-ing ice, all crinkly, and when Daddy took me there a few times, I could see the deer comin' to catch the browze early mornin'.

"You could never see a flaw in the main house. The stairs were polished every week. The niggers used to be afraid of the stairs and some of the floors. Not because you could slip, but because you might see your face in them. Niggers are afraid that if you see your face in anything that isn't like water or a mirror, you'll never be able to see your face again.

"You can't really see your face, or even an outline, in a shiny floor, of course, you can only say, 'Why, I think I could see my face in that. But we had two maids that wouldn't look down and where they were going, and one broke her leg and the other hit her head so hard she couldn't work for a week.

"I never did read many books," she went on, in a voice that dreamed, and Madi could tell that Halsey was dreaming. "I never did," said Sarah, "but they were all there. Daddy's library was incomparable. From the central hall you went down two steps into the library. Isn't that right, Halsey?"

"That's right!"

"It was an oval room, with gray paneled walls, cut from cypress. You used to look in there and see Daddy with all those books, and he was always reading something. The only time you'd look in there in the evening was when he was in Washington. Daddy was a senator, but he always liked to get home and settle down and read. Isn't that right Halsey?"

"That's right!"

Just as Madi was about to despise Halsey as an echo he put his hand firmly over hers as it lay on the sofa beside him and said, "Sarah Bruce. A long time ago it seems to me you started to tell Madelaine that you wanted to speak something honest. How long is it going to take you?"

A dreamy expression slid down Sarah Bruce's face. She had looked younger while she had been speaking, but now the youth receded, and her cheeks were gaunt and two strings emerged on each side of her throat. Her eyes were haunted and then they were not haunted any longer. They filled with a tide of purpose, and her body stiffened in her chair.

"As I said, Madelaine, I'll be very candid. I didn't bring you over here to have dinner and talk about the children. It didn't take me long the first time I met you to tell that you could do for the children anything that could be done now.

"I'm not goin' to ask you for any reports of any kind. I'm going to ask you to help us. We want to know where Jeb is buried. And we want you to help us."

It was such a direct, honest, unflinching blow that Madi was staggered.

"How could I help?"

"We know he's here," said Sarah Bruce, "and other people know he's here. Elvira knows he's here. Howard knows he's here. Harte Trace knows he's here. Jenkins knows he's here." She broke off and stared at Madi.

"But how could I help?" Madi asked.

The strong lips of Sarah Bruce curled. "I don't suppose you will help," she said scathingly. "I don't think you know where Jeb is now, but what would you do if you did? Keep your, I suppose, nice little behind in a tub of lard, or tell us? What would you do?"

Madi found it hard to look into Sarah Bruce's eyes. She could remember all too well her wish that Jeb Trace would not be found this season.

"Why don't you look at me?" Sarah Bruce said.

Madi's face came up and her eyes; her attitude was present behind the act. "I was thinking," she said, "that I liked my whatsis to be in a tub of lard or butter. I'm sure I have never gone through the things that you have, but my own have been enough for me. And I must admit I find things very well here, prison or not."

"Then, you want to protect yourself, is that it?" asked Sarah Bruce.

"I think you misunderstood me. I didn't say that."

"Are you going to tell us what you might learn, or not?"

"I'm not going to be your spy."

"Not even for a decent cause?" asked Sarah Bruce.

"I don't know what the decent cause is," said Madi, "because someone is lying."

"You don't think we lie, do you?" Sarah Bruce said, standing up.

"I don't know."

Sarah Bruce walked to her and slapped her face. "You'll have to understand," she said, "that even when you can't make up your mind, then you're calling somebody a liar, and it could be me. I want your apology."

"I will give you nothing."

Sarah Bruce's hand raised again, but a swift hand moved out and deflected it, and it was Halsey's. His soft voice had a vein of iron. "We won't do it that way. Even if it means we don't find him, we won't do it that way."

He took Madi by the arm and gently lifted her and escorted her to the door. "You didn't wear a coat," he said.

"It was only a short walk."

"You'll use one of Sarah's."

"I think not."

"I want to talk to you, and it would be best if you had a coat, scarf, and gloves."

"I think not."

She was staring over his shoulder at Sarah in the firelight.

"There's no soul in a coat," said Halsey. "It's just some material to put on, just as walls are some material to keep you warm."

Madi did not know whether to believe that he really felt that; she had heard—from whom was it now?—that he was superstitious and even believed in the ghost Sarah.

"I don't want her coat," said Madi.

"It's any coat," Halsey said, as he wrapped her in it.

He opened the door and she shivered in the cold air and hugged the coat around her. It was not far to the cell block and her room and why should she suffer it for a woman who had slapped her in the face?

They walked through what she had heard had been a flower and vegetable garden for prisoners. It was ruts and plant rubble now. The light was fairly good here from a half-moon. Elvira had told Madi that the maniacs had planted roses and the soldiers had planted tomatoes.

They came to a small inset door in the stone, and Halsey took out a long key. "This hall goes up to your tier," he said, "but if you are not afraid, I'd like to show you what we have been doing."

"At this time of night?"

"This is the best time of night for you," he said. "When, during the day, could you explore the caverns?"

The answer was that there was little possibility during the day that she could do so, and even if there were, she would have to ask the permission of the colonel.

"Do you want to see them?" Halsey asked.

She did not want to see them. No prisoner wants to see the prison that is worse than his own, because he does not wish to know the depth to which he can descend; and yet that was a falsehood, she knew. Every prisoner would like to know how far he could descend, and how far other prisoners had descended in comparison to himself.

She knew it was hopeless to protest. It was not the feel of his urgent hand on her arm and the mystery implied: what he wanted her to see and what he wanted to say to her.

It was more than that. She had been, and in a way still was, a prisoner. She must see where her friends had lived.

"I will go with you," she said. There was a feeling of softness and reluctance in her flesh, a fine line of stress, like fingers on an edge.

He opened the door. She had expected a rush of dank earth air. Instead, there was cold, clear air.

She heard a rasping sound, the strike of a match, and a lantern was lit. He lifted the lantern. It was an old-fashioned kind with a wick doorway in the front. She had seen them before and had imagined they were little houses. A brass and glass doorway for a small animal that would stare out with an odd air of proprietorship. The rasping sound must have been from the hook on the wall behind him. Beside it was another hook, holding another lantern. The walls of the hall were moist. There were two directions that could be taken, the hall to the right or the stone steps directly ahead to the left of the wall and the hooks. "This way, Madi," he said, and turned to the stairs.

She stood a moment, unmoving, the air from behind her against her, and the breeze that rose from the depths below. He had paused on the first step below her. "Close the door, if you will?" he said.

Still she did not move. A magic thing had happened: he had called her by the name she knew herself by. She could not remember how long it had been since she had been called "Madi" except in personal identification in her own mind. She could tell now, thinking about it, that the lack of that identification of the name that was herself was like knowing yourself in the mirror without having anyone else know what you looked like. How many years had it been since to someone else she had been "Madi"? It had been a long time since her mother had called her that. Her mother had tended, in travail, to become more and more formal, as if formality itself could remove some of the taint from their lives. As things had become difficult, her mother had stopped using the diminutive and had, finally, always said "Madelaine." As if the dignity added stature.

Along this route to becoming nameless, in an intimate sense, Madi had been unconscious of any concern she had about it. Until Halsey called her "Madi," she had not realized how much she missed it. The most intimate contact she had had for a long time was with Harte Trace, but he had never called her "Madi," nor even "Madelaine."

There was a gallantry in Halsey Selby; she had known it when he did not drop her hand, and she knew it once again. He did not show impatience, he did not wave the lantern; instead he held it ready with a steady hand. He did not blink or command. He waited. He knew something had happened, and he did not ask what it was. He gave her the time to compose herself. He was thinking of her, and not of his own purpose. Or was he trying to befriend her for a secret purpose?

She drew the door closed behind her and followed him and the light down the narrow winding stair. She did not know whether he was a real friend, but she had to know.

She was not a large girl, but nevertheless she had to bend her neck a little on the stair and turn her shoulders. As they descended, the current of air increased in force. She avoided as much as possible the light he held fairly high considering the low ceiling, and the light showed wide black cracks in the left wall. There was seepage in all the cracks and trickles from mortar between other stones that had not parted. The occasional sight of a pouring spout of water, one of them pouring across the back of her neck, made her think that springs or some other sort of pressure were on the other side of the wall.

They came to a long, flat table of stone, diminishing into distances beyond the light. She felt breathless from the bent position she had had to adopt, and from the strange, too airy constriction of the place. She shivered and huddled into her coat.

"Why is the water dripping that way, Captain?"

"I'm not a captain." He smiled at her; the slow effortless smile. "Can you call me Halsey?"

"If you wish."

She wanted to call him "Halsey," but there was a resistance to it. Regardless of all she had been through, she was hopelessly naive. It was not easily conceivable, but the truth of it was there. Death, torment, jail had not reduced something in her that wished to make things, people, statements seem as true as they were obviously intended to be. Intended to be but might not be. She wanted to call him "Halsey," but why did he want her to? There was a liar or liars here, and she had no inkling of which they were.

"There was a cistern through here at one time," he said. "A mountain water-catching device. If you ever had some occasion to study military history, you'd have found that military engineers were always building that kind of system. Then other people took it up for places like this. To have enough water was always the reason. It was always done in areas of this sort. With some sort of stone conduit inside the fort, and some vein of stone to the outside, with a stone intake. If I remember my history a little, I think one of the biggest in the old times were the cisterns of Hadrian. Do you remember that old boy?"

"We never met," she said, and wished she hadn't been flippant.

He laughed, glancing at her through the golden light that in some way seemed affected by the gray-brown stone, as if the stone wanted to sleep and were resentful. There was an aura here of fatigue that did not want to be disturbed.

"I met him and a lot of other people," said Halsey. "I suppose if I had time, I could be quite a historian. But life turns around and looks at you and asks a question. The question always is, what are you going to do now? And when you know the answer well enough, you put everything aside and do whatever it is that has to be done. Someday I'll be an old man, and the things that have to be done will have to be done by somebody else. The only question is, when that happens and I have time, will I be able to use it properly?"

His gentle, deep smile was on his face, but she saw through it once more, or thought she did, into a deeper place where there was a passion. It was not difficult to see the passion emerge in his sister—Sarah Bruce could not restrain it for long. Her manners broke down before it, as there was seepage through these strong stone walls. But there was not much, if any, seepage through the visible walls of Halsey Selby. But she knew there was; she had seen him riding with Confederate uniform and flag and saber around the perimeters of the prison. That mad passion, walled in his politeness, soft voice, and manners showed her a flame that was crisscrossing the bones of his chest and would eventually want release.

Thinking that, as she looked into his eyes, she hated herself. She knew what the release would be that Halsey would want. A double, a triple release. To find Jeb Trace. To relieve his sister's mind at last. To fight Harte Trace.

She wondered what diminution of the soul she had attained during her tribulations. All she had been caring about was that she was comparatively happy here and she had not wished it to be disturbed. Sarah Bruce had seen through her, and Halsey must see through her, or else why would he have her down here?

She could see through herself and had earlier. And yet that did not change anything: she did not want Jeb Trace found, not this season. She would think about it again next year.

These people were making a human being out of her again by contesting for her, and when Jeb Trace was found, they would forget her and kill each other and she would have nowhere to go and no person to be. A tired, frightened person was inside her skin, pushing against it.

"I've been thinking about the cistern system," he said, his smile leaving his face. He lowered the lantern to his side, and as the light passed his mouth and cheeks, she saw a compulsive seriousness become lines there that quickly aged him. His voice traveled into the ceiling dark, and the cold air made her pull the coat tighter around her.

"I don't just want to knock these walls down and let the water out. Seems to me there's enough water in there so that the bones, if they're there, would just be washed away or be pretty hard to find.

"What I want to find," he said, "is where this water came in when the cistern system was used. Now, this water came in somewhere. We know where it came from outside. I understand you've seen it, you thought it was a quarry?"

"Yes, the children showed it to me."

"Yes, and now Jenkins and Howard are putting a fence around it. Almost finished with it."

"Yes, they have."

"I have no cause for combat with that. There ought to be a fence around it. Nobody can go down there and dive in the water and come up in here and find the outlet. That's all been blocked up somewhere. And the exit is sure in hiding.

How do you hide a place where a water supply as big as that came up? How do you do that?"

"I don't know."

"Somebody around here knows," said Halsey.

"Do you think the men got out through the cistern?" asked Madi.

"I think they tried to," said Halsey. "I think they made it most of the way and then something stopped them. They're here. They're nowhere else. We've looked at everything else. And I've explored every place here they could have gone except the cistern. And I can't explore that unless I know where it came out, not where it went in, that's too far away. Nobody could swim that far underwater to come in here and find anything."

"You brought me down here," said Madi, "so that you could try to convince me that I should help."

He did not drop his eyes. "Sarah Bruce is patient but not patient enough. Least in moments. She'll go on with this for the rest of her life if necessary. But she has those impatient moments when she does things in the way she did with you, the slap. If we want you to help us, we can't do it that way."

"And you're not impulsive, Captain?"

He smiled, long-eyed, ironic, secret. "Calling me 'Captain' is supposed to put me in my place, because I'm not a captain. You might refer to the day you arrived here and I rode the charge against this fort. I heard you saw it. You can't whisper much around here without everyone knowing it. The niggers in the kitchen pick it up and take it to Auntie Close.

"I rode that way that day, not because I'm impulsive—I'm a pretty deliberate man, as you might find out someday. I rode that way because I wanted Harte to know I had found something he wouldn't have wanted me to find.

"When I rode that way, he knew I had found something. When I didn't show up to fight him, he knew I hadn't found Jeb. But he knew I had found something. I'll show you what I found that day."

Madi felt an ache at the back of her head but preferred to ignore it. Halsey took her hand. There was nothing gentle in the way he took it now. They went along a long corridor, narrow, dry, with acrid rising dust under their feet. They came to a door that Madi thought must be ten or twelve feet wide. It was oak and in two sections. There were iron bands across the top, the middle, and a foot above the

92

bottom. The doors opened outward. Halsey grabbed the edge of one side of the doors and threw it back against the stone. It was a cannon-sound in the confines of the place.

They walked inside, the lantern showing facets of dull machinery that beckoned and loomed. Beckoned? Madi saw a down-portion of a treadmill that came from a well of the upper floor. Halsey led her to the trap that opened beside the mill. The trap was open. He glanced the light down into it. Atop a gray-green mold of grain there were some black, shattered bones.

"I would have believed," said Halsey, "that some animal had gotten in there by mistake. But rakin' around, I found a bone with a ring on it." He went into his pocket and came out with a cheap gold and artificial emerald ring and showed it to her. "That's the kind of ring," he said, "some girl, some little girl somewhere, would give a soldier as a token."

Madi could say nothing.

Halsey said, "Somebody down here got himself into a loaf of bread. Not Jeb, of course. Officers didn't work in such places."

"You don't think Colonel Trace——"

"Sarah Bruce has been checking records for two years. Ten men were supposed to have escaped from here, and nobody ever heard from them or found them. Over a hundred men died. Only seventy of them have dead records. Nine men came in here and didn't die and didn't escape. Where are they?"

She did not think she wanted to know. But she looked. Into corners. On walls. The mystery of looking around for a mystery that was silent in a place where the mystery had happened and had not been a mystery then, but was only a mystery to those who tried to find out what had happened.

She could remember Harte Trace kneading her neck, but she could not think of him kneading men into bread. She did not intend to extend the thought into the obvious conclusion that some of the men's comrades would then eat them in the bread. She did not intend to, but it worked itself out that way.

She would have forgiven herself if she had gotten sick at the thought. What else could you decently do but get sick at the thought? But she didn't.

The only thing she got was a strange wondering about what Harte Trace was doing and thinking upstairs at the moment.

Old bones and rusty grain did not make the present appear anything less, nor the past more savage. She realized then that graves did not truly lift up their contents. You thought about them because it was expected of you, but it was not warm and alive and close. If you were alone it was, because you had nothing else. She had not been alone since she had arrived here.

How immoral could she have become? "You see," said Halsey, "there's the possibility that a man was murdered here. Pushed into this thing. It could have been an accident but maybe it wasn't. That's what got me so mad I put on the uniform and rode around this place. I had the idea that a man was murdered here, and maybe a lot more."

"You can't be sure," she said. She was looking at the treadmill and up into the crotch of the ceiling from which it came down, and the heavy rusted iron gears below it and the grinding stones, flat and serrated and silent. The ceiling was broken by a long stone tube near the treadmill and at the bottom of it was a long open pan; on either side of the pan were wooden counters where the dough for the bread must have been kneaded. She probably knew the answer then, but did not want to. The answer was in the ceiling of the bakery room. Her mind accepted it and put it in a drawer, and she would not refer to it unless she was forced to.

She looked down at the floor.

"Does all this bother you too much?" said Halsey.

"We better look at something else."

"There are a lot of things I want to show you. What're you looking at over there?"

"That must have been where they made the bread?"

"Yes, that's right. They got the water out of that wooden fount there. They had to draw it up. That's one of the three internal wells here, this one drawing up, the other two with the pump."

Madi knew it was not a well.

They were deep in what she had called the bowels of the earth. An accurate description. A horrid one. Dirt and stone corridors and cells along the route. They had gone down into three successive tiers of cellars. They were deep below the ground now. No wonder she had not been able to hear and had not been shaken by the explosions Halsey had made. It was very silent below the earth. She had thought it would be very damp. It was not. They had passed through a damp area, and then the dampness had vanished within a layer that she thought might be about ten feet. It was cold and iron down here. He showed her the cells where frost never came and where warmth did not either.

"It was like preserving vegetables," he said, "in case you wanted to use them some other time. Can't really let them rot, or they wouldn't be any fun anymore."

His sepulchral levity did not make any impression on her. She had left a good part of herself (was it a good part?) several layers up. Now all she had was the coat wrapped around her, which he had told her had no soul in it. It was only a thing. She was glad she had the thing, and she was glad that nothing of the passion of Sarah Bruce was in it. She doubted that the passion of Sarah Bruce would live long down here without a fire. She huddled herself together. It had been a long time since she really had felt well. Somehow fatigue was becoming more acute.

Could they have missed it? "Did you always do the work down here, Mr. Halsey, and Mrs. Trace the work up on the top?"

"You'll find my name is Halsey after a while. Why, yes, Sarah Bruce has done all the checking up there, and it's been a lot of work, and I've been excavating down here. The tunnels they made and some they might have. We gave ourselves a division of labor."

That would be why they did not know. Neither one of them had seen both the top and the bottom.

She was shivering, and there was no use in telling herself that all of it was from outside herself. It was cold down here, true enough, a kind of cold she had never known before. A buried cold, an eternal cold. The cold at the unchanging bottom of the sea. But it was nothing compared to the cold that came from deep within her. The cold around her was dead, inanimate. The cold that came from within her was as alive as flame. It was a flame of ice. It brandished spears that cut without cutting. It was something that you could not easily die from, therefore there could be no surcease from it. It was like a sharp knife that could cut you forever, with all the pain of sharp cutting but none of the ultimate unconsciousness.

It was baffling to be up against its edge.

What did you really know about yourself, after all, even though you had known yourself all your life? And all this so

95

monotonous, one cell after another, with the rotten straw for beds lying there.

She wanted to hide from herself her information, and hide it from others, that she knew where the internal outlet of the cistern was and that the outlet contained a secret, or else it would not be disguised as it was. It was no use trying to explain to herself that she wanted to protect a life or two by keeping her discovery a secret. It was hard for her to imagine a duel actually taking place between Halsey and Harte Trace. And yet why should such a possibility seem difficult to imagine? They might not think that Harte Trace would be willing to duel, but she thought they were wrong. He had a sense of honor, he was a romantic, even if he denied it, and he had proven by strangling her that he was not as averse to violence as people seemed to think. It was no use trying to explain anything to herself; she was sure that the only thing she wanted to protect was her own comfort, her own sense of being.

The knowledge, real or self-imposed, made her furtive. This was a good atmosphere for it. The dirty underground cells and tunnels reeking of past and feral life seemed to try to hide themselves, like beggars who recognize a friend of better days. She began to feel at home down here, too. There was a furry horror on walls here that her mind could not divorce from the family relationship to the walls of her brain. She conceived a furry horror in there and, by so doing, made it exist.

She would have loved to have turned Halsey to her and have said with suberb honesty, "I know where the outlet to the cistern is. It's in the room upstairs, the room of the treadmill. Near the treadmill is another ostensible mill, or press, with wooden bearings, a cover, and turning spokes. It's circular. But it isn't a mill or press, it's the disguised cover of the cistern."

She would have loved to have said it quietly down here, honestly, looking into his eyes. But what would happen? It would be all over for her. Couldn't she forget that? Did it matter? Did she really consider it that much? Or did she consider it much further?

Did she consider his slanted eyes changing? His mouth beginning to curl. So far down here he had sometimes shown gleams of his native humor, an ability to laugh, a resiliency that must have stood him well in the war. He lived with the outlined memory of horror down here and yet he did not brood down here, upon evil, death, and misery. Youth, humor, and a supple but fierce mind were evident all the time. They walked on in the simple monotony of prison design.

"Now, here's a cell where a boy was thinking about things he shouldn't have. His mother was home with the Bible on the table, knittin' things for him, and what was he thinking about?"

She looked at the marks on the wall and knew what the boy had been thinking about.

Halsey laughed, in that soft but outpouring way he had, a big, controlled laugh, a strong laugh under mastery of his throat, and she thought he was going to touch her, but he didn't.

Could anything but a calm, confident mind find the humor in a deep cell like this where a young man had been thinking of young women that he might never meet, at least on this earth? And it was not callous. "He could draw in a sensitive way," said Halsey. "He was doing poetry there, in a way, the kind his age might require."

"Do you know who he was?" Madi asked.

"His name doesn't matter," said Halsey. "He left who he was here."

But at the door of another cell he put out his hand for a moment so she could not enter. "I don't want you to see this one, but I'm going to if you're willing. That's because what you asked before is true. We want your help and we're trying to win you to the cause. As I said, Sarah Bruce is getting impatient, but that don't mean the cause is a bad one. So I'd like you to see this so you'll know once more about the conditions here. That's one side of it. But the other side is that I think you're a girl who is sensitive and can imagine a lot. You'll be able to see that an animal lived in here, and you'll be able to see, without any explanation from me, what might have made him that way."

She touched his arm with her fingertips, and his arm dropped away from the entrance.

In the lantern light the cell was a golden gray-green. A thick, hoary fungus was growing over the walls, emanating from behind a large wooden shield. The shield must be very thick. A hole was bored into it to the depth of about a foot. A very rough hole. She doubted whether she could remain sane for a matter of minutes if locked into this place. And how long had the creature trapped here been here? How strange to call him a creature. How long had it taken him to know that that was what he was?

97

The only implements he would have had would have been his nails and teeth? Isn't that correct? His nails would not have lasted very long. Most of the work must have been done with his teeth. He had to get out of here. Of course. No human being, or even a partial one, could stay in here. Some sort of slimy living thing could prosper in here, but not a man or a thing that remembered being one.

He became an animal in the futile attempt to become a man again. He must go upward, somewhere from the slime, so it could not claim him and take him back across the long struggle that had been accomplished long ago by the race and that he must, alone, attempt to accomplish again, without the help of eons and generations. And the iron was impervious to teeth and nails, and the stone, so he chose the wood, and his compulsion was bitten deeply into it.

"Now I want to show you my camp," said Halsey.

"Camp?" said Madi. She was feeling a definite headachy pain between her brows.

"Why, sure." He took her arm unaffectedly. "The first thing a soldier, if he's going to be a good one, has to know is that it isn't indecent to be comfortable. Fact, it's a requirement! You hear all that historical talk about Sparta and all, but they didn't accomplish much. The Roman legions subsisted on some wheat grain and wine. That's all the soldiers got except when they were real good, and then they got some salt. But Rome fell.

"There're a couple of things a soldier has to learn, and he has to learn 'em immediately. One is that a soldier has to be as comfortable as possible—that builds up his inner reserves. And then he has to know there are reserves behind him, so when he fights, he has to issue it all. There's some comfortable man back there waitin' to come in and tell him to go back and sleep.

"We knew all that and we would have won if we had any possibility of getting any little part of either reserve. You can't have a reserve if it isn't there."

The cell he took her into had a great hole in the rear stone wall. No air came from it. Instead, a stagnant depth smell. Halsey lighted another lamp, then extinguished the one he was carrying. He explained, "You never go into the dark without knowing where there's another lamp. I have them all over here. And as soon as you come to the next lamp, you put off the first. That's so you don't forget and think you

98

have a clean lamp when you don't. Do you know what could happen to somebody down here if the lamp went out?"

"I expect so," she said. "I was never in Oregon, but my mother was, and she told me about the blizzards. She said a person could walk out the door to see how things were and turn around and never find the doorway again."

"That's the way it is in a place like this," said Halsey. "That's just the way it is. You become disoriented. That's an army term. Orientation is knowing your way around. And what you've said is the way it is."

Besides the lantern he had turned out, she saw the one he had lighted and another and a box of candles and a roll of canvas and woolen bedding, and a box that looked like a ration box, and standing on top of the box a bottle of whiskey. There were also shovels, picks, small, tight boxes that might be explosives, and a pile of metal woven mats, like ancient armor, that might be those he used to cover explosive charges. There was a table cut down so that you could sit before it on the floor and various designs were clipped to it.

"Do you live down here?" she asked. She was appalled at the prospect. An icy harm was slipping up within her, until her throat was cold.

"No, I don't. But sometimes I get pretty tired, and it's cheerful to have a camp to come to. If I went up to the top, tired that way, and laid down, I wouldn't get up again and come down. But when I'm down here, I do it easily. Besides, if there was a cave-in or anything, it would cheer me to know I could fight my way out here and have something here to warm me up."

"I notice there isn't any air coming from that hole over there."

"No, none at all. That goes in pretty far. I didn't like goin' in there, but I figured if the boys had worked that hard all the time it must have taken them, they should have somebody appreciate their efforts.

"I went in all the way to the cave-in. It must have taken them all. That probably accounts for some of the people we can't find. Things of that sort. I would have started digging in there, but I'm here to find Jeb, and I knew he wasn't there. I found a pair of boots that were regular issue, Confederate. So I knew Jeb couldn't be there. Jeb had irregulars, cavalry. In other words, they provided for themselves. In addition to that, this isn't a compound prison. In a compound prison, you can't help but have officers and enlisted men together.

In a cell-segregated prison that isn't done. So there's no chance that Jeb is among whatever men are out there in that cave-in." He smiled at her. "Are you going to help us?"

He opened canned oysters. The sight of the canned oysters made her sure that she would never tell him anything. He brought a dark bottle of wine from a musset bag, pulled the cork, poured for them both, and said, *"Voila!"*

He was purely a suspicious person.

As he plucked an oyster from the can and gave it to his mouth he laughed at her. She had always felt that she knew what he was laughing about before, but now she could not be sure.

"Would you like an oyster?" he asked smoothly.

"I don't think so."

"Don't you like them?"

She did not know. She had never had an oyster. And it was horrible that such luxury could happen in dungeons.

"I don't want to eat them all myself," he said.

"I would prefer not to have any oysters," she said.

He filled two small, round glasses with the dark wine and handed a glass to her. She did not want to accept it, but his hand stayed before her and did not waver and he did not speak, so she accepted the drink. A small, dark glass of wine in her hand, in a fine-cut glass, in the deep dungeons of a prison?

"Drink," he said.

"It seems indecent," said Madi.

"In some ways it is," he said. "But it isn't in all ways. Remember that the men here would have loved to have seen a pretty woman like you down here, and would have loved to have seen her drink."

"I doubt that," said Madi.

"Then, you doubt everything about men," said Halsey. "Most women nowadays don't know what we are. Women are so used to gathering their clothes around themselves for fear somebody will see something that they don't know that a good part of a man's time is spent in other pursuits. I've never known a good fisherman or a good hunter who was doing what he wanted to that day who would look up if he had a bite or something in his gun if somebody sounded a trumpet and said, 'Here comes the naked goddess.'"

"I don't know what you're talking about. It's irrational. I said that I don't think that the men down here would like the fact that I drank."

"Then you misunderstood me. I meant that your decorum

wouldn't matter to the dead, nor to the living either for that matter, if they were in here. They wouldn't look at you sitting here and having a drink as something dissolute. But as something alive. And most women aren't. All dead faces, as they have been taught to be. The only time a man wants to be with a woman is when he wants to have something he can find with relief."

"You have me trapped down here, Captain, and there's nothing I can do about it."

"I guess you like that idea," said Halsey, "but I don't strangle women and then start to rape them and not finish the job."

"What?"

"I told you there aren't any secrets in a prison. There's always some listener who thinks he can make things better for himself."

The hundreds of thousands of pounds of the prison above were on her head. It came to her that that was not something she had not experienced before. In this prison she felt the stones; in the jail she had felt the people.

"I would like to go upstairs," she said.

"If you would care to," he said, "I recommend you to the corridors."

She thought. The corridors. The number of stairs. The turnings? "With a lamp?" she asked.

"A lamp wouldn't help you," he said.

"Why did I have a feeling that you would say that?"

"Because you know there isn't anything else I can say. But I'm not going to let it go at that. Sarah Bruce got disgusted with you too fast. You didn't get the point. You should get the point and get it easily, but since you can't, I'm going to have to make it for you.

"We are down here together," he said. "We do not suffer. Or do we? If we do, can we add it together? Can we find a way to make suffering a thing you can suffer? That's a possibility. I've seen it.

"You can't tell me your heart is calm. I don't know much about you, but I don't need to. I've been in the field, in a losing battle, and when I look into a person's face, I can see whether they have to retreat.

"You have to retreat. You have no other choice. You have to pick somebody and hope it's the right one. The somebody isn't yourself. You've already done that, and it doesn't work. You have to pick somebody else, and I guess you ought to be thinking about it about now."

She stood up. Her knees felt surprisingly weak!

"Would you mind being taller than I am, sir?"

He stood up.

She slapped his face. "I would not want to have to leave that in my will to your family," she said.

Halsey laughed. "I'll give that to my sister for you if the time ever comes when she bothers me enough. You're shivering, so sit down and drape some blanket over your feet. The cold down here is a lot more sly than the kind you find up above. You don't like to be teased one bit, do you? Know why I was grinning like a fool over the oysters?"

She was cold and disliked him, and he was as improper in his attitude down here as would a man be who sang a ribald song in the middle of the church service. But his face was so open and candid now that she could not be sure. Was he being ribald? Or was she being as pious as the people are who have reverence for the suffering they never experienced themselves?

She wanted to sit down, wanted to forget her hauteur or temporarily put it aside. And she had a better excuse than that: she could not get out of here without a guide and she might as well submit to the fact and make the best of it. Besides, the cold was beginning to force her to want. It was difficult to subscribe to a haughty attitude when you felt yourself becoming, even only to a slight extent, the creature that men down here must have become, far beyond the unpleasant sights and personal sensations that she had undergone in jail.

She allowed him to implore her to sit down, and she sat down as if it were an imposition. She allowed him to bundle blankets around her as if she were patiently submitting to insult. She allowed him to give her a canned oyster, and she made a wry face even before she had decided whether she liked the thing or not.

He was giving her his grinning leer as she swallowed it. What did he expect that she would do? Forfeit her dignity by throwing up? She would not allow that to happen, no matter what the expense.

There was more than one way to throw up, she had learned on two occasions in the jail when she saw a sight that prompted that type of explosion. You could throw up outside of yourself or you could do it inside yourself. The former disgraced but relieved you; the latter kept you secret and private, and very sick. The latter was the better.

She waited as he grinned. Nothing happened. The oyster

102

...ad a quaint pleasantness but she found that she was not as ...ungry as he had predicted. She kept her eyes from wandering to the can, her nose from smelling the barbecuing food.

She felt insolent down here. There was no rank or station ...n this place, any more than there would be between two ...eople on a desert island.

"May I ask what you're grinning about in such a devilish ...ay?" she asked.

He burst out laughing, slapping his thighs. "Madi, you just ...ade yourself a fallen woman!"

She stared at him. "Is there supposed to be some quality in ...ysters that does that to a woman?"

"No," he said. "It isn't the oysters that does it. It's gallan-...ry." He had stopped laughing and had become reflective. ...As I said, I study up on lots of things. Always have. One of ...he things I took note of during the war was logistics. ...ogistics is the art of having the right amount of something ...t the right place at the right time.

"I didn't have any business cluttering up my mind with ...hat sort of material because we didn't have any logistical ...roblems. Just like a man with no money doesn't have to ...orry himself about where to invest it.

"If you don't have anything to transport from one place to ...nother except yourself and your horse, you don't need to get ... headache worrying about what you'd do if you wanted ...wenty tons of food to be in a certain place in Tennessee on ... certain date.

"Unlike us, the North did have problems of that sort."

"You overcame yours," she said, "by taking the widow's ...ast chicken!"

His face darkened. It was so swift, it was astonishing. One ...moment there was a good-humored face. The next moment ...here was a graven mask of fury. Incongruously, out of the ...nask of fury came a placid, low voice. "People spit asper-...ions," he said in a voice so gentle that it was frightening in ...ontrast to his face. "A man in my command took the works ...rom a widow's clock in North Carolina. Two hundred men ...new he would never need that clock, and he never did."

There was silence. On a number of occasions she had ...hought she had heard silence. There are various brethren of ...ilence. Morning in a small town, morning in the city. Silence ...ver a gray coffin, a silence that exists for you no matter ...what sound is around. Silence in a cell. The silence of ...lespair. The silence when your ears must reject everything, ...ven the voice of self. The silence made more known by the

103

rustle of a claw, the skitter of paper, the beat of a heart, th sigh in a corridor, the tap of a heel, the brush of rair the glimmer of light in the dark, the fleet, unknown bu familiar sound, the breathless silence of waiting for somethin, pleasant. The silence of fear, and that of the beating hear

This was the first time that she had heard the silence o passion. It was like listening to a soundless thunderstorm Knowing it was there and hearing it without hearing it, as i you were deaf in the midst of it. She could imagine it wa like standing above immense surf crashing over rocks an having the sound torn away from your ears by a powerfu soundless wind.

She looked past his furious face and burning eyes to th soundless mouth of the airless cave.

A pristine ice was creeping through her, her head ached She was tired. His passion seemed childish. Her tirednes came from a far point. Tired from childhood?

Her icy fatigue made her mute.

"Are you all right?" he asked, feeling her hands.

She did not have to answer that she was not all right. Sh was sure that he could see that she wasn't. How long had i been that she hadn't been feeling all right?

"I'll help you up," he said.

It did not matter. For some reason, nothing matterer anymore. The deepness of the place she was in had beer pushed aside, in a light, airy feeling of intimacy with him, as i their picnic had been held on the side of a mountain, nor inside a mountain of stone.

The depths had begun to appeal to her. Once she and her mother had taken a train into New Jersey to visit some dir relatives, and when they got off the train and walked towar the farm, there had been a caravan of gypsies beside a creek Madi could remember the dirty nails on her sleeves, the dark-eyed appeal, the ghostly, mad longing. She had fel queenly and eager to help them, and appalled. As she fel now. The depths were fingers on her arms, and she wished tc have warmth for what was here, the unwritten memoirs o prisoners, the rhetoric of Halsey. She wanted nothing. Sh wanted to sleep and see morning again. This was not a nice place when you used elementary addition and subtraction.

She did not want the fingers of these depths to appeal tc her. She did not want Halsey's. But she did not protest when he helped her to her feet.

"You're very cold," he said.

"Very cold."

He held her close to him. It did not help.

"Come along," he said.

Insensate corridors.

They seemed to be rushing. They seemed to be standing still. They were going so fast, and they were not going at all.

Her head was airy with a clear, cold blue wind.

She knew she was a very sick girl.

⌒⌐(CHAPTER IV)⌐⌒

HALSEY WAS CARRYING HER, AND his boots boomed over the stones of the rotunda. She shivered against him, as close against him as she could get considering that she was swaddled in his coat. The booming of the steps was a command from down in there where they had been. It was an echoing call from deep down. She huddled into her covers in ineffectual escape. Something in her was answering the call from the caverns. He had taken her out of there, but not all of her. A part of her was lying in despair down there in rags on a cold floor and her teeth hurt and gray-green garments were sewing themselves or growing themselves to her aching toes and after a while her face would itch with it and it would move through her hair and she would be all of it and it would be all of her.

Her eyes were not able to close, as if points of ice under the lids scratched when she tried to close them. Her eyes felt glassy and hard. There was some sort of determination to see, or a determination not to see what was in the dark when her eyes would be closed to the waving motion of the lantern that was hooked over his elbow.

Her weakness was so profound that it was more of her than anything that had ever been Madi before: more than cold skin and chilled brain, more than lips, more than memory. As much, she knew, as becoming born, almost as much as being dead. There was almost nothing else but fatigue. Everything else was glimmering. Weariness was an infinite dark lake, and on its surface and in its perimeters small lights shone and parts of her flicked like tiny fish and disappeared.

The closed cells they passed were peopled with invisible dark figures of ice. They were not there but they remembered.

She was on her cot in her room and swaddled the more. She heard the thrust of a poker, the rattle of coal, in dual light of lamp and lantern. Her lids were partially closed now. Hot fatigue was melting the shards of ice and her lids were slipping down, and points of knowing were in her eyes waiting to escape. In those points of light were cavernous histories she did not want revealed to her. They were the lanterns held on a highway in front of a caravan of approaching dreams, an overwhelming host still at bay in the darkness of her mind, if she did not allow her eyes to close.

Now his light was swinging above her. He towered and shrank and fell away; he was a ship. He was the helmsman in a storm and she was the watching ship and would drown soon.

"Forgive me," he was saying. His words were the waves, lifting high and falling back, and she was riding on them. "I'll go and get someone. Forgive me, I made it all too much." His swinging light and his shadow, his form, moving and fading away, and his steps, and she was alone.

A cone of ice detached itself from the dark on the wall above the shimmering light of lamp and fire. Although she was not told, she knew that the ice approached in friendship and a burning supplication.

It was comforting that Sarah was here. She could help carry the burden, and she was wiser and knew it much better. They could cower in the icy tears together and peer out through secret apertures under paint where marks of fingernails were dimless eyes in the faceless stone.

She had gathered an effortless force, as simple as lying in sunlit water, and had carried her shapeless form, deep in her covers, into the air over the stove. And pieces of cold, like needles, were drawn from her body and she could hear them fall on the floor with a clinking sound. When the needles were withdrawn, they left small, stinging wounds. The wounds were quite hot but not really uncomfortable. All in all she had executed an intelligent maneuver.

A morning lifted behind her eyes. It was warm and flower-yellow, but there was a blemish in the center of it. This troubled her and she allowed her lids to raise further so she could examine the impediment.

Elvira was bending over her; Elvira's face was quite different when you looked up at it from when you looked straight at it. When her face was looking down at you, the eyes had large bags under them and wrinkles were forcing themselves upward from the chin. Her grin made Madi think of a large pouch.

The mouth of the pouch opened and words spilled over Madi's face.

"You're here, you're here, all snug, with Howard and me. Yay-es. You didn't expect that fancy southern belle to take care of you, did you?" She laughed heartily and, since she was still leaning over the bed, she gave Madi a preview of what Elvira would look like if the undertaker was not particularly expert.

"Why, she don't think about you or anybody else." The twang was a happy harp. "You're a human being here, and we'll prove that to you. Yay-es.

"You've been in delirium. Have you ever heard anybody in delirium?" she asked, gaily. Perhaps she was remembering past interesting times.

Madi's lips were cold and dry. They worked to become flexible. She answered weakly, "Yes." But there was nothing weak in her suddenly; wariness was not weak. The wary were strong because they were ready.

"Delirious," said Elvira, smacking her lips. "I've had a lot more to do with that kind of thing than Howard. Howard's kept himself apart a lot. He never really did the work that got you right in there. Howard never saw the things I have. When we brought you in here and I could tell you were going to be delirious, do you know what I told him?"

"No."

"I said, Howard what do you think of that young girl? Isn't she sweet and nice? He said you sure are sweet and nice. I said, Howard, wait until you hear some of the language she knows. Great goodness, he couldn't believe it. Howard has a very placid nature. Nothing much that's happened around here has ever bothered him. But he was shocked!"

Her broad, pleasant face was pleased. "He was shocked." Her shrewd eyes rested gently on Madi's. "Do you want to know anything else you said?"

Looking into the gleaming shrewdness of the eyes, Madi felt a native counterattack begin in her, an inner shrewdness rise from its waiting place and sit like a lawyer beside her tongue. And yet she could feel the naive skin over the bones of her face. A sense of triumph came to her. She was shrewder than this woman, because hers was not merely shrewdness, invisible; it was caution without malice.

"It isn't necessary to know," said Madi. She was lying deep in a soft bed; she was asprawl. She was weak. She had just come awake. The room was bright and warm. But her defenses were ready and apparent. She could be proud of herself. It did not hurt her to know it. It made her feel as if she was poised in brush to spring if need be. She did not

108

know what she wanted to spring for or at, but she was prepared. The night in which she had been defenseless, the woods in which she had been stumbling were not fully around her now.

"In a way," said Elvira, "over the years I've been a nurse. I've done a lot of nursing in my time, and here I am doing it again." She preened, self-satisfied, well-fed, the morning light making her round cheeks shine. "Most people are curious about themselves. Yay-es. They want to know how they acted and what they said."

"Did I have a doctor?"

"Well? We thought we could do for you. You were only exhausted. I've done a sight of nursing. Great Lord, yes. I managed you. You didn't mess much, and I took care of it. Nobody can accuse me of being squeamish, no matter how tidy a house I keep. Howard's a little that way, squeamish, that's one reason why we don't sleep in this room. This was the room where the little Jew lived, the maniac. Remember me telling you about her? Howard and I sleep in the old attendants' room. Both rooms are about the same."

Elvira's hand touched Madi's forehead like a hot iron.

"You're nice and cool," said Elvira soothingly. She folded her hands in her spread lap and sighed. "You couldn't have gotten any better care anywhere than from us. We opened the door to you with joy in our hearts.

"It seems to me," she said, with beaming laughter, "that this is your year! Do you realize how many people have received you with love! As we have, as Howard and me. You're one of us, part of the family. And that's one of the reasons why we didn't call anybody else in. We want to do for ourselves here. We want to give everything possible. What greater glory can there be than that? And then there can be happiness for all!"

She flooded Madi with a love-face, large and glistening. "I have something cooking for you," she said, as if it were a conspiracy. "Howard will come in for a moment," she said, "to see how you are." She paused at the door and looked back fondly.

Madi expected her to throw a kiss, but she must have forgotten.

Howard came in sniffing like a hunting dog. "Do you smell what I smell cooking out there?" he asked.

She couldn't smell anything. Her nose had a rime in it and she hoped it wasn't green.

"It smells wonderful," she said.

It was amazing how suspicion could give you more strength than whatever treasure Elvira was cooking. There was a point when you went down, no matter what your strength; she had seen it happen to her mother, and it had happened to herself, but some bodily substance, care, warmth, and you could return. And when you did, you seemed to have a part of what was taken away from you when you would have been an easy victim for anything.

She hadn't known before that this worked mentally, but she had seen it work physically. In one of the tenements in which she and her mother had lived she had seen a beer drayman carried off to Bellevue Hospital on a stretcher. Before he had been taken away very ill, he had been a big, ruddy man. When he was brought back, he was an angular sack, his face pulled inward by a sick suction so strong it was devouring him.

In a few weeks he had come downstairs again, a big, ruddy man, congratulating everyone on the fineness of the weather. He hadn't had to start over again. He had become exactly as he was.

"It's been one of the happiest events in Elvira's life," said Howard. "She's had a very hard life. We've always had to work for anything we got. And we never had any children." He looked into space. "I guess Elvira was pretending a little while she was nursing you." He regarded her keenly. "She was with you night and day. Your life has been hard, too. That made us closer to you."

"You can't possibly know my appreciation," said Madi.

He took one of her hands into his two immense flounder hands. "Gratitude comes straight from the Bible," he said. "Straight from the Bible. The good fisherman.

"You're welcome here now, and you'll be welcome here anytime in your whole life. And that's no exaggeration!"

"Howard, get off the girl's bed. Do you have some young ideas?"

"Only toward you!"

"Puff! Now get my robe and put it around her shoulders. Madelaine, this tray is something. Yay-es. Now sit up. Howard?"

"I'm gettin' it, I'm gettin' it."

The soup was an experience. If their characters had had the integrity of the soup, she would have loved them.

She ate all of it and smiled and lay back. She was weak, but she managed to look weaker. She let the woman bow the pouch over her and kiss her cheek. She allowed the flounders of his hands to protectively hold her delicate hand for a moment. She returned their love as they gave it to her at the door. She lay back and closed her eyes as they went out.

She had changed. Or, if not that, one facet of her nature had wished, or been compelled, to take prominence over others.

There had been many lights in her. This one was cold and alert like the smile on her face as she began to sleep again.

There was an afternoon sleet against the two small windows. Looking back over her own forehead, she could see how small the windows were. In order to get out of those windows the girl who had been held here would have had to be no girl at all. Wraith.

It was a wood stove here, crackling. She wondered why there was a stove in the room at all, unless Howard had installed it while she had been unconscious. She looked around; no, it was a firm wall stove, here and active for a long time. Maybe Elvira and Howard had guests. She could not imagine them keeping a stove in fine condition for no reason.

She felt strong enough to sit up. She wanted to see the icy sleet. Pellets were flung. It was nice to have glass on which things could happen. She had been some time without it. And there had been cracked glass. With ingenuity you could minimize it.

She could not remember anything after Halsey had left her in her cell except the beginning of her delirium. The impression that Sarah had joined her had come back today. Not that Sarah had joined her again; instead she had wakened for a while with a pity that Sarah could not join her in the warmth she possessed or that possessed her today.

She did not believe in Sarah, the ghost, as a person, present, as an emanation. She believed in her as Halsey did: that she was there because she had been there, and her having been there was so important in the way it had happened that she would always be there. It could not be otherwise. Sarah was there.

If she appeared to you in the beginning of delirium, it was because you would want it so; you would want to be as the legend. Sarah had delivered the men toward freedom. You could free them, too, in a lesser sense, by having them found and given decent burial, not to be nameless somewhere underground in soil they must have hated.

111

She lay back; the windowed sleet was flinging itself strongly. Elvira came in and put spice cake and tea on the bed table. Elvira was tiptoeing on feet so small for such large breasts. A pebble fell against Madi's cheek, and her eyes opened to see Polly Ann sitting on the chair and eating a piece of cake. A crumble of the cake must have fallen on Madi.

"Caught!" said Polly Ann.

"The hungry one," said Madi, mostly to herself.

She had wondered before and she did again about Polly Ann's prerogative: "It's nice of you to come to see me first."

"I'm the biggest," said Polly Ann, devouring the cake. "Is it all right if I eat this?"

"Yes, please do. Am I going to have any other visitors?"

"The other girls are going to come and see you."

"Why not leave them a piece of the cake?"

"They won't mind," said Polly Ann, eating the cake. She did not lick her fingers. She held them in her lap as if they were leashed.

Elvira came into the room, went to Madi, touched her forehead, and fussed with the bedclothes. "Oh, my goodness," she said, "I don't think we should have let you have visitors so soon. You're cold and wet. Polly Ann, feel her!" She took Polly Ann by the hand and put the hand close to, but not touching, Madi. She pulled the hand swiftly away and made the suggestion: "Isn't she cold?"

Polly Ann pulled her hand away. "That hurt."

"Oh, my dear, I'm so sorry, I don't want you to get sick."

"Will I get sick?" asked Polly Ann.

"Come into the kitchen and I'll give you more cake. I'm sure you'll be all right."

"The other children want to see her."

"Not today, Polly Ann. You're the big girl, and you can tell them how sick Miss Brooks is. Come along, I have a lovely cake, and you're the big girl. You can tell them exactly what you think."

The door closed. Madi knew how strong and clear her mind was, but when she tried to get up, she found that her body had not yet made the convalescence his had made for the beer drayman. She fell back on the bed before she had gotten off of it. She was getting up again when Howard came into the room, and said, "I'm sorry you can't see the other girls. I'll talk to you and keep your spirits up while Elvira is having cake and tea with them."

"My spirits are fine, and I'd like to see the girls."

112

"You wouldn't want to frighten them, would you?" asked Howard.

"Why would I frighten them?"

"Now, you mustn't get fussed up," he said. "Do you know how sick you've been? Elvira's kept you as quiet as possible. You're all awake now and think you're strong, but you're not."

His face was lazy, clear, and smooth. He was already younger-looking than Elvira, and perhaps was, but as time went on he would look younger and younger in comparison. She wondered if a lazy life was a kind of health resort.

"I think it would help me to visit a little with them," she said. Her stubbornness was instinctive. Was she testing?

"Elvira knows best," he said.

She started to sit up and he pushed her slowly back. She was surprised by the strong determination in the big hands. He must believe everything Elvira told him.

"I'm a little weak," she said, "but I'm not really sick anymore."

"They'd make you nervous," said Howard. "Do you know how nervous you've been?"

"I've had a right to be nervous—" she began, but stopped, knowing she had made a mistake. His face became tense and watchful, unlike the familiar Howard face.

"You can be calm," he said, "very calm. Elvira's done a lot of nursing. Trust to that."

A knock at the door, and then Elvira peered in coyly. "I don't want to catch you two in anything!" she said.

"You flatter me," said Madi, and knew she had made another mistake. Elvira was still coy, but the stare was blank. Not unfriendly. Blank. Impersonal. The inner expression of guards and nurses, ministers and social workers. Only bill collectors seemed to be aware of conflict and get heat into a situation.

"Yay-es," said Elvira. "Of course I flatter you, my dear, or I wouldn't be married to him. The little dears have gone. How children can eat. Howard, I'm afraid there's only a cut of cake left for Madi——"

"I'm a meat and potato man," said Howard, standing up.

He left the room and Elvira amply filled the chair. "Positively no visitors!" she said, as if tendering delicious news.

"How did Polly Ann manage it?" Madi asked.

"Polly Ann!" said Elvira, as if the name were an epithet. "The poor little soul. I wanted her to see you so she could

113

know how sick you are. I told her that I knew how badly she felt because of it, and that I'd make her feel better. Anytime she wants, she can come to the door. I've told her of all the goodies I have for her."

Elvira sighed. "You're in my care. Howard's and mine. I've talked to everyone. It's agreed. I didn't expect the children to try to come in, but Colonel Trace don't have the best control over them. But I have the situation in hand now. I do indeed.

"Polly Ann will get her goodies, poor little thing. Liz won't want to come back, poor dear. She's always so worried. Worries whether her mother has money. Worries about school. There won't be another teacher, at least for a while. At least until they leave. She worries about Auntie Close being a Negro. But she's bright, that little girl. You might not think so, but I know so. I'm practical. I worry. I do the right thing. Good walls, a fire, food, those are the things. Liz knows that. She's practical. Like me and Howard. But Howard leaves it to me. I told Liz it wouldn't be practical to come back and see you, because derangement is sometimes contagious. She has enough worries, poor little thing.

"Yay-es. Marcy. How that child dreams. I guess as her teacher you know she does practically nothing else. How she used to dream about that cistern pit. Do you remember her thinking about the cistern pit all the time?" she asked slyly.

"I remember."

"You're so abrupt. I suppose because you're not well. I suppose you'll get nicer as time goes on. As you feel better. After they leave, you can have some nice walks. Howard will enjoy that. He can tell you everything about what happens around here, the seasons, the flowers, animals. There isn't anything he don't know. Well!"

Elvira plumped herself down more in the chair. She sagged as if it were a joyful activity, like dancing.

"Marcy has some dreams now. She'll spend all her time using them. I told her how you thought you were Sarah the ghost, or Sarah was your friend—it was hard to know which you meant. I told her about the nail marks on the wall, and Sarah being willful and having to be whipped.

"I told her that she could look at the place where Sarah was whipped. I'm going to show her. I told her that Sarah was all right and didn't get whipped unless visitors got her disturbed and made her act up. I told her that Sarah dreamed beautiful dreams when she was alone and nobody bothered her."

"And Colonel Trace will never know all this when the children cavort and talk at dinner?"

"You are willful, aren't you?" said Elvira, pityingly. "In the first place, my dear, they are southern girls and he is a northern gentleman." She stood up, smoothing belly and skirt. She said archly, "Do you think they would tell him anything, even if their poor little souls could?" She paused at the door. "Would Colonel Trace worry?"

"Elvira!"

Elvira wagged a finger at her. "You must not be naughty. You've acted like a lady. You are not a lady. I don't like high and mighty ways from prisoners."

She closed the door and turned what sounded like a large key indeed.

Tension, suspicion, confirmed, weakness, fluids, sickness, taunting had aroused the need in Madi and she looked for the elegantly concealed slop bucket Elvira had provided for her room in the prison. Nothing concealed such an object.

It wasn't under the bed and it was not on the ceiling.

Perspiration was flowing through her nightdress and she was staggering. She felt as if her bones were pushing through her flesh, and her skeleton would appear in a mirror, if there was one.

She knocked at the door of her room. They did not answer. Her knock was long and thick and dull. It was a door you would find at the end of your last street. There was nothing to reach on the other side.

The pelting on the windows had changed. You could hear nothing now except the imagined brush of the snow, brushing wings. Snow butterflies. Now was the time to compose poetry. Sit down at the table, find pen and paper and write light verse about snow. Like moths. The moths lifting up and that evening dying. Write it. Write it! Write it, think it, write it! While the things down there told you you were going to be an animal soon if they wanted to make you one?

A trickle came down her thighs and she squeezed her legs.

Her weakness had transformed itself into a passion, and the passion had made her falsely strong.

She was not going to be a cat or a dog on the floor. She beat on the door but there was no answer.

Her leather trunk had been put in the room and she busied herself putting her clothes into the wardrobe and the drawers. Could she batter the door down with anything?

She beat a chair against the door and the chair fell apart

and the door remained the same. Staring at the door, she saw there were other marks.

In a fury she beat at the door.

She swung the wardrobe around with frantic strength and shoved it against the door. The door didn't even slacken against the lock. She tore at the handle of the door. Her nightdress was ripped and she had torn herself on something. Blood was flowing down her right arm and already was encrusting around her fingers.

She beat the windows out with her fists and tried to crawl through one of them. Tears and blood flowed down her face.

She would not lose her honor and humanity, never, never, never! She ran to the open empty leather trunk. There was no other place. Successive waves of nausea emptied from her, and she was dizzy and slipping. What had Elvira put into the soup?

Her fingers gripped the edges of the trunk. She hoisted herself up and over and fell forward on the floor.

The door of the room was forced open and she dimly perceived the long curls of Colonel Trace.

"I told you," said Elvira, "I told you she's mad."

"Oh, my God, oh, my God," said Harte Trace.

"I'll take care of her," said Elvira, "I'm used to these things. She's in my care, Colonel. In my care."

ᑎᕞᐸ **CHAPTER V** ᐳᕐ᠆

"**I DON'T WANT ANYTHING TO EAT,**"
said Madi.

"You have to eat or you will die," said Elvira. "Yay-es.
Now have this good soup."

"What did you put into the soup the other time?"

"It was Howard's suggestion. Do you remember I told you
you had only messed yourself a little and I did something
about it? I told Howard, and he said it was unnatural. You
might need a little something. I put it in the soup. I'm sorry
and Howard is sorry that it happened when we couldn't hear
you.

"We were out cutting wood. There's a lot of coal used here
but the colonel pays for it. When they all go, we won't use
coal anymore. That would be silly, wouldn't it, with all the
wood around? Howard always says he's going to cut the
wood, but if I'm not there with him to make sure he does it,
he's always doing something else. He takes a gun along and
that gives him a good excuse to sit down and do nothing. He
can always come home and tell me that he wanted to get
some birds for our dinner. If he ever does, I can guarantee
you'll get some for dinner."

"Are they all going to leave soon?"

"Wahl, we hope so. Just too many people around. This is
our life here, Howard's and mine. Hunting, a little gardening,
our nice snug cottage, don't you think it is?

"I wish Howard would do some farming, but I guess he
won't. It don't matter. They'll be leaving, they won't find anything, and the colonel won't sell the place or rent it out. I
suppose he could make it an asylum again or sell it to someone who wanted to make it a prison and hire out for contract labor.

"But the colonel don't want to do that. It's a tomb here. He
wants his brother to rest.

"We'll caretake for him. He can afford it. A lost monu-
ment from the war, up in the mountains here, and nobody

117

will know or care. Howard and I have caretaken since the war and we'll be doing it again.

"It'll be better for us now, though, with you here. We didn't get cash before. Just the use of the place.

"But the colonel is a man who can't stand any pain for people. That's why he has Jenkins on his pension list. Howard and I have always been envious of Jenkins, until now. We have knowed that Jenkins would never have to worry. Colonel Trace with his cavalry was riding past a farm one day down in South Carolina. Jenkins was watching them and came up to the fence, as I understand it, and offered to volunteer.

"Jenkins had a blind mother who walked up to the fence and said if her son wanted to go, that's what she wanted. Colonel wouldn't hear of it. But between Jenkins and his mother, the colonel let him go along. The mother died, I guess, you never hear otherwise, and Jenkins got shot and lost his voice. The colonel has a heart that nobody could forget. That's why we're lucky, me and Howard.

"We won't only have this place all to ourselves, when they leave, we'll have a pension. Howard isn't any good at it, but I am, and I've already talked to the colonel. Yay-es. He's going to pay us enough for your room and board, so we'll have some profit. I told him that bringing you here slipped your mind over on the other side.

"When they all go, you'll be happier. I already told you that you can have nice walks with Howard. It started this way here, as I told you. And that's the way it's going to be. I guess this place was meant for it.

"Places are meant for things. You can't get away from it. Since I was a little girl," Elvira said, sentimentally, "I've heard yelling and screaming around here. At first I used to think it would be nice if it never happened. But you get used to it. It's home. Howard and I took a trip one time, and it was lovely country, but I almost went out of my mind. It wasn't home."

She bent and kissed Madi on the forehead.

"You'll be happy here after a while. Especially when they're gone."

Madi sat up.

"Howard?" said Elvira in a trilling voice.

Howard came and lounged against the doorway. He was smoking a cigar. "Colonel left this for me," he said laconically.

"Halsey will come and see me," said Madi.

"Halsey?" said Elvira. "Howard, Halsey is going to come and see her."

"He took care of me," said Madi.

Elvira nodded. "He didn't give you to that sister of his. He knew better than that."

Howard laughed loudly.

"He knew better than that!" Elvira said appreciatively.

"He knew better than that!" Howard echoed.

"How's the roast?" asked Elvira.

Howard shrugged indolently. "That's not my job. You get through talking to her, and then you look at the roast. I'm getting my fishing equipment together for tomorrow."

"Can you fish in this weather?" asked Madi.

"Ice fishing," he said, and turned away.

Elvira said, "You can't get close to us by asking questions that try to get you intimate. The only way you can get close to us is obedience."

"I didn't want to get intimate. I didn't know people fished through the ice, which I presume it is."

"You're a willful girl."

"I'm goddamn what I wish to be."

"You are a filthy girl. You've proven that. No dog, horse could be dirtier."

Madi scrambled up her arms and was beaten back, and then was sorry that she had provoked an attack that made her less again.

Elvira was panting. "If you do that again, I'll call Howard. He's very easygoing, but he wouldn't let that happen. Howard won't let anything happen that could destroy our comfort."

Madi was panting. The woman's strength had been too superior.

"Do you think Halsey will come?" Elvira asked, her tongue sticking out gray, her cheeks bustling. "Don't you think he knows that the colonel was under your clothes? Jenkins and the kitchen niggers know that. Slut." Elvira took her by the hair and pulled it. "Slut," she said again.

"I guess she is," said Howard, standing in the doorway.

"She's fighting back," said Elvira.

"Why bother with her? Nobody's going to come. The children won't. You know Mrs. Trace don't care. Colonel knows she's insane. Halsey only wanted to use her and thinks she's a slut. Why don't you let her alone and come out here? I'm going to get up early and go ice fishin', and I don't want this aggravation!"

119

He slammed the door.

"Do you see what you did?" said Elvira.

"You're not going to tame me."

"Dear me, what rough talk. Tame? We're going to nurse you into health, no matter how long it takes. And since you don't want this soup . . ." She took it up and went to the door.

"Don't dirty up again," she said severely. "There's a commode under your bed. Learn to use it."

Madi sat up and got out of bed. Elvira dropped the tray on the floor and came forward with fat purpose. She took Madi's hands, twisted them behind her, and threw her down by kicking her behind the knees.

"Howard!" she called. "Do you want to see the pink and white ass of a lady who shits into trunks?"

After a while Howard stood in the doorway placidly eating. "No pimples," he said.

"Do you want to see her get up on her hands and knees?"

"I don't want to see anything. Why don't you just keep her?"

"If you want to see it, I can do it for you."

"I don't want to see anything!"

"Is that the way it is with you? I was wondering what you'd do when we kept her here."

"I'm eating!" he said.

Elvira threw the covers over Madi. They went out and closed and locked the door. Madi was dirtier now.

There were winds crying in the nights. This did not surprise Madi; how could the winds do anything else? Ever since she was a little girl she had known that the atmosphere around you adjusted itself to the way you felt. If you were happy, the rain was; if you were sad, the trees allowed their leaves to bend their heads. Even deep sunlight would order itself to your mood: if you were depressed, the sunlight was a ferocious glare; if you were exuberant, the sunlight danced, chasing mild shadows with brooms.

She understood enough about institutional life to know that these people might not experience any personal satisfaction in torturing her. Some of them did, of course, but others did it by rote: to break the spirit, subordinate the body, command the mind. It was training, designed to make the process of keeping jail a less difficult chore. It was the process of putting a muzzle of shame or fear on the fiery teeth of a person who wished to rebel toward freedom.

It was often as exact and educated as the knife of a surgeon. It was an operation! It was meant to excise courage.

Lying in bed, very weak, she wanted to think about Sarah, and Jeb Trace. Nothing had managed to break their spirits. She wanted to dream about them. She needed salve for a horrible wound, and they were the ones who carried it in their hands.

They were here somewhere. Who could know it better than she? In her weakness she was calm. Sarah was disobedient and defiant, and Jeb Trace with his long, flowing hair was laughing and watching. He and Sarah ran laughing through the passages, defiant.

Her hunger strike began that evening. Elvira came in with a steaming tray. "You'll find out how nice we can be to you," she said. "Never in your life have you tasted Maine hash like this. Howard was originally from Maine and he loves it. Won't let me touch a drop of the work when it's hash. Has to do it all himself. Now sit up, dear."

Madi did not.

"Do you feel weakly? This hash will change all that. You'll see. Howard spends hours over it. Mostly people throw hash together. That's garbage. But not Maine hash. Sit up, dear." Her voice stiffened a little. Madi did not sit up. She was looking at the ceiling and Sarah and Jeb Trace were dancing a jig. What else?

Elvira put the tray on the table. "It'll get all cold," she said bleakly, "and Howard worked so hard on it."

"He shouldn't have troubled himself so for me," said Madi.

She did not have to look to know that Elvira's face would become congealed suet.

"He wouldn't go to all that trouble for *you*," Elvira said.

"I thought not," said Madi, "so let's not pretend."

"The way you like things is the way you'll have them," said Elvira, plucking up the tray. She also gathered up the water pitcher. "Do without! Your music will change its tune. But you'll have to pay the piper. You'll pay the piper!"

Madi was glad that Elvira had picked up the pitcher of water; the act had pronounced a decision on Madi's part. She wouldn't accept water either. Nothing.

From what she knew about the human body, a person could go a great length of time without food, but only a brief time without water. How long? Days. How many? She was not sure. It was a mighty and solemn thought. Days. She had never measured time so realistically before, even when her mother was dying. She had known her mother was dying but the process was one that did not seem as if it would truly have such a culmination. There was always tomorrow.

Now she was going to deny herself tomorrows. How would her strength combat theirs? She had allies. Sarah and Jeb would help her.

In the morning Elvira came into the room, her face a boiled potato, her mouth a sullen smile. She carried the smell of eggs.

"If you don't want to sit up all the way," she said kindly, "I'll pillow and spoon you. Oh. I've done that so often, nursing. Do you want me to do that?"

Madi was thinking deeply. This thought that she had in mind was one of such gravity that it called for all her powers of concentration. These people had to know that they had something in their cottage that they might not be able to cope with. The reason they wanted her here was to be able comfortably to cope with life. They wanted a docile ward, for whom they would receive remuneration that would simplify their life and make the future secure.

They were not going to have such a person, nor such a life.

"The eggs are getting cold, and you must be thirsty," Elvira said, the sword of the virago on the cutting edge of her words, but only threatened.

"I don't want to have to call Howard," said Elvira.

Madi had come to her decision. It was a momentous one. Regardless of how they had used her, regardless of where she had come from, she knew that they knew she was essentially a gentlewoman. The rich Colonel Harte Trace, an aristocrat, would not have hired her for his beloved nieces if she had been otherwise. She would not have eaten with the colonel and the children if she had been otherwise. She knew that they knew they would never be invited to the colonel's table. And they would never have a lifelong pension from him if he did not feel that she was a gentlewoman who deserved the care.

They had to know that they had here an implacable wild soul who would not perform within the prescribed boundaries of her class or nature. Who could not be broken by humiliation. Who could cross the borders of her inherent decency and expected decorum, despite the things to which she had been subjected. They must find a wild gypsy who could not be humiliated enough to become easy, ever.

122

With steady menace Elvira said, "I'll have to call Howard."

In a steely but everyday voice Madi said, "Fuck you."

Elvira staggered but didn't drop the tray. If the word affected Elvira as much as it affected Madi, it must have had an effect bigger than the walls of the prison. It took as much of a leap over convention for Madi to form that word and utter it as it would take leg power to leap over the fifteen-foot wall.

Through the screen of her lashes Madi saw the word break into the woman's conception of the possession she was holding here in this room.

Elvira had easily been able to force Madi into desecrating herself—but this word had not been forced upon Madi. She had spoken it herself, from conviction, without coercion.

"I won't listen to anything like that," said Elvira, and went out with the tray and closed the door. She paused a few moments on the other side before the key haltingly turned in the lock.

In late afternoon Elvira came with tea. Madi had plumped herself up against the pillow. There was the damp of weakness between her legs and in her palms, but she said cheerfully, "Dear Elvira, good old servant. What have you brought me on your knees this time?"

"Knees? We're independent people up here. We none of us have ever been on our knees to anyone."

"I'm sorry to have struck your sore spot, Elvira. I'm sure there's no trash up here like there is in the South."

"Trash? A filthy thing like you dares to call us trash?"

"I didn't call you trash, Elvira. I'm sure that you and Howard have eaten and drunk with the colonel, Mrs. Trace, and Halsey many times. Halsey insisted you call him by his first name, of course. If he'd insist that I would, he'd insist that you would.

"I apologize for calling you a servant. You're not a servant, you're a nurse. Now, put the tray across my lap and I'll see what you have for me." She snapped her fingers. "Quick, woman."

Elvira slowly shook her head. "Nobody does that to me. Nobody has ever done that to me. You're going to have to say please. Yay-es."

"Put that tray on the bed!"

Elvira backed off toward the door.

Madi pled: Sarah, Jeb be with me in this next moment.

Madi flung back the covers, sprang from the bed, and spun Elvira around as Elvira turned to hurry through the door. Elvira was far stronger, she had proven that—but Elvira was not in balance with events. Madi was able to spin her around, lift the cover on the muffins, yell, "That's shit," and flip the whole tray over, hot tea scalding Elvira's legs. Elvira screamed. Howard came running.

"She's insane," cried Elvira, "she's insane."

Madi knew that she was in trouble. She hadn't had the opportunity to put Howard in his place, and judging from his advancing terrible and purposeful anger, he hadn't heard Elvira being put into her place.

But Madi had forgotten in the moment what had happened earlier—the "fuck you"—and Elvira had certainly told him.

He came on, furious. Madi held out a straight finger and pointed at him. It was an instinctive, hopelessly arrogant defensive, like holding up a cross in front of a gorilla, but it implied something to him, something enough for him in his unthinking rush to think and hesitate. And Madi saw he was confused, staring at the altered arrangement, at Elvira crying and saying, "My legs, my legs," and the spilled tea and muffins, and he stared at the imperious, slender white, arrow-pointing figure of Madi.

"A lady like you," said Howard, "a lady like you, saying and doing the kind of things you do."

His face was gray and shocked. He had been willing to watch her being degraded from outside herself, but his mind could not accept the fact that she would be able to do it from within.

Howard took Elvira to him and led her out as if she were a broken doll. At the door he looked ruefully at the broken possessions on the floor. His face was flushed and he didn't look at Madi, nor did he pick up the broken things. She saw he had the impulse to do so, but he would not bend.

"My nice teapot," said Elvira.

The door closed. Madi waited for the key to turn in the lock. It took a long time, and then it turned as if it should not be heard.

Exhausted, she lay on her bed. Now she knew the answer to something that had puzzled her when she was reading French history.

When the other aristocrats had ridden in the tumbrils through the streets of Paris to the guillotine, the citizens had taunted and reviled them and thrown things. When Marie Antoinette had ridden the tumbril, the streets of Paris had been silent.

Marie Antoinette had scratched and shrieked.

No matter how much people could hate what they considered their betters, they expected them to take it all with dignity, not the way they themselves would take it.

That was the weakness of the fierce people who considered themselves inferior. If they became ashamed of you, they could not find any hope for themselves. As if a dog found his master fighting with his mouth at the same dish. Where was there to go?

Elvira and Howard had hoped to tame a gentlewoman, depending on her need of dignity, violated enough already, to make her tractable. And then they would lead a long, gentle life and give her everything they could and never molest her, as long as she was good. And she would have to be good to preserve her place. That they could take away.

But Madi had helped them take it away and would not try to replace it.

Madi had wondered whether they would try to force-feed her. Or hold her nose and pour liquids down her throat.

She was drowsing in the dark, and the fire was long out. She was not thinking of food, she was thinking of rain, and you extended your hand and the rain beat against your wrist. You held your hand there awhile and then put out the other hand, and the rain fell and clung to the veins and turned around in swirls and poured through your palm and over your fingers. You could lick your fingers if you wanted to.

They didn't come in as mean-broth; they came in joyously. Bearing fire and other gifts, including themselves. They smelled of cooking and powder. After only a short while there was tart wine, touched by light and fragrant spices from a pewter dome.

Stoic, she sat up in bed, seeing the blue veins in her crossed hands. Her hands were very thin and she was going to will them to be more so. Sarah and Jeb had not, she was sure, such a latter-day possible feast. But she would go their way in the same way they had—without it.

"Guess what we've got for you," Elvira said chattily.

"What?"

"Wild duck!"

"I see."

"Howard's done them," said Elvira.

"You're going to like these," Howard said.

"I've done my part," said Elvira. "Nobody can say that Howard is the cook around here."

"Except for the best cookin'!" said Howard, still poking at the fire.

"Howard shot them at the upper pond," said Elvira.

"On the wing and the right way," said Howard. "You don't ever have to worry about getting some shot in your teeth when I shoot."

"No, Howard's an expert," Elvira said. "He's a woodsman. Didn't I tell you he could tell you about everything around here? The seasons, the animals, the plants?"

"I sure can!" said Howard.

"You told me," said Madi.

"Yay-es," said Elvira. "Now, shall we have wine first?"

"I don't want anything," said Madi.

"Child," said Elvira, "you haven't eaten or drunk for so long. You don't want to get sick. You know you don't."

"She ain't going to let herself do that," said Howard. "You're talking to a lady who has some sense."

"Oh, she's been a trial," said Elvira, "she's been a trial."

"Let her get a hold of herself," said Howard. "Do you think you, or most people, could go through all she's been through?"

"I don't know how she's done it," said Elvira. "That's what I don't understand."

"You nor anybody else," said Howard.

"Let's eat and drink and be cheerful," said Elvira.

"No," said Madi.

"You've never eaten anything like this," said Howard.

"I don't intend to eat or drink," said Madi.

"You're bein' kind of foolish," said Howard.

"Let me talk to her, Howard," said Elvira. "Miss Brooks, I've never held back on anything I've said. Yay-es. Isn't that right, Howard?"

"Right as rain."

"Miss Brooks," said Elvira, "you might think that we were being cruel to you. That's what it must have seemed to you, but that wasn't the intention."

"There was no intention to continue that," said Howard.

"I said, let me talk to her, Howard."

"I'm willin'."

"Then, shut up!"

"I'm shut. As a matter of fact, I'll take all this back to the oven. I don't like waste."

"Go back to the oven and shut up. Miss Brooks. We were only trying to protect you and ourselves. I think at one time Howard told you how happy we were to have you. We never had a child. We wanted one, back into the mists of time. Way back, in those mists where everything begins." She rubbed a blue hand against her eyes.

Madi thought coldly that the tears seemed real enough.

"You're a very willful girl," said Elvira. "We had to try to protect you against yourself. We had to get you here so you could belong to us."

How maternal and paternal, thought Madi.

Elvira wiped her eyes. "You don't know how we prayed for a child."

More for a pension, thought Madi.

Elvira lifted careful eyes that were shrewd and intelligent.

"We'll let you go," she said, Out of an apron pocket she took a big key. "Here's the key. We did our best to keep you, because we want you. We want you for this place, for the pension, and because we want you. You have the key now. Think of where you will go. Is it a kind world? Has it been for you? Yay-es. I've cleaned your trunk, and if you want it in the morning or any other time, you can have it.

"Howard?"

"I've been keeping it hot."

"Bring in everything, Howard."

He put the duck, wine, and whatever else it was on the table.

"Are we invited to dine with you?" asked Elvira.

"Take it all away," said Madi.

"We'll go to bed, Howard," said Elvira.

"Now, you know, honey," he said, "that that's all I ever think about."

Madi did not dare eat anything they had left for her. It would be very easy to get rid of a difficult girl and convince Harte Trace that she was still there. The smell of the food was agony. Her tongue was so dry that it seemed to want to crawl into her withering and die.

She looked at the key that had been left for her. She padded to the door and tried the handle. The door moved slightly against a bolt. She threw the food and wine into the fire.

ᴖᴖᴖ(CHAPTER VI)ᴖᴖ

"LOOK AT WHAT YOU LOOK LIKE," said Elvira, holding up a mirror.

Madi stared into the face of a mummy. It was hard to remember that that dry, wrinkled face had been young not so long ago. Madi tried to smile at herself, but not only was it too much effort, the folds of skin did not want to comply.

"Is that the way you want to look?" asked Elvira. "A pretty girl like you. That's the way people look in the grave, and some of 'em just before they get there.

"Oh, my, I've seen that face so often. It's what's called a dysentery face by the army. The poor soldiers. All the water drains out of 'em from the backside and they begin to look like that. And then they look like that for all eternity. But they can't help themselves. They can't. You just can't stop that water from draining out of them when they have the dysentery. Out back there, out in the graveyard, why there's a lot of them in there because of dysentery. It's called the prison, or camp, disease. Do you want to lie out there with them, looking like that, a pretty girl like you?

"Think of all those handsome boys out there and how they would of loved to keep the water in them and had the bloom on them, rosy cheeks and bright eyes. If they'd been able to keep the water in 'em, they'd have gone home long before this. They'd be married and have little fat children by now. Why, some of 'em could have two children by now, and a third one coming, if they'd taken any pride in their work. And don't you think they would of?

"Why, a person is like a plant. Off over toward Madlinson, over in the hollow near Springer's, the wells went dry. The plants and flowers and grass all dried up. A tomato was a little crippled thing, all wrinkled up and not fit to eat. We rented that place for a while when I was a little girl. Two years, as a matter of fact. But you couldn't depend on the wells. There's nothing but dying when there's no water.

"Here you are lying here with your teeth closed and won't

take anything into your mouth. It almost seems as if you've got the lockjaw. When we try to do a good Christian service and hold your nose and pour it down you, you won't let it go in, it trickles down and you get purple. Don't you know how childish that is, like a tantrum? It's just like a tantrum. Howard and I were talking about it.

"We want to be your benefactors. You think you're better than us, and maybe you are, but we've never been in jail, as prisoners. Maybe better people than us have been in jail, but it wouldn't make us proud to have been.

"All we want is to lead a nice gentle life. That's all we've ever wanted. Howard and me. He's lazy and I'm only a woman. There isn't much a woman can do to bring body and soul together. You do all there is around you that you can, and there isn't anything more than that." Her fingers touched Madi's. It was a remote sensation, beyond a desert.

"I can tell," said Elvira, "from touching your fingers you were a seamstress." Madi had helped her mother sometimes when the work was at home. "That isn't the queen. What're you going to do with what you've learned out of books? Where're you going to take your table manners and your straight back? To prison? To another job like this? Maybe not in a place like this, but the next place would have a wife, the lady of the house, and then you don't think, do you, you'd sit at a colonel's table like you're so proud of here?

"The colonel might fumble you, like this one, but it would be in the pantry or behind a bush.

"Do you think I don't know your mother went to a pauper's grave? I can read, and the colonel's a military man and keeps all the reports he gets."

Madi would have wept in that moment if there had been any juice for it. Luckily there was not. Her dry, aching eyes stared implacably into the woman's litany.

Elvira asked. "Don't we people who can have nothing have to grab every apple that starts to fall from the forbidden tree? Maybe you've gone around thinking that the fruit of the world ain't forbidden to you—but it is. Because you're a lady isn't going to give it to you. Yay-es. Haven't you found that out by now?

"A lady's only as good as her father's money. When there isn't any of that, she isn't as good as people like me. I can at least marry Howard, or a good farmer, if I was lucky, but who would want you? Who would want somebody who's so much better than they are? And the people who are good enough for you, who you can eat with, they only want you to take care of the children. Unless they want to fumble your clothes 'tween-times."

The pain in Madi was of a different kind than she had ever known before; it turned out that body chemistry had something to do with emotional pain. Before this she had known two kinds of pain, the one that spent itself with a storm of tears, and the one that contained the hot, passionate reservoir of tears.

But this pain was one in which she was dragged, a limp, dry branch, over seared stones, and her flesh was soft and limp with rubbing sand in the creases.

"The colonel will send us money," said Elvira, "and all three of us'll live here. If you decide not to act so proud, there're young men in the mountains here. If you want to stay proud, teach school. This's a nice cottage, and me and Howard don't mean any harm. We never had much of a chance. Howard's Howard, and I can't do it all. And what would you expect of me, livin' in a place like this, all my life maniacs and prisoners? Do you think I was like this when I was five years old? Everybody in the countryside said Elvira was one of the happiest, brightest children. Did you know I was called 'Vira of the sweet voice'? I was. Yay-es. I had a gifted soprano. People came from miles around to the church services. I used to sing here at the prison when one of the boys was going to be buried. I know all the old sentimental songs. When Johnny Comes Home Again, Tra La, Tra La!"

Madi's coated tongue made her think of the gray-green fungus that came from the bitten wooden shield in the dungeon over there.

"There's no young preacher around here now," continued Elvira, "but the one we have, least in the decent church, is well along. There'll be a young preacher around here one of these days, never fear. I can see you pourin' tea for the social ladies and doing the visiting. There ain't a girl in this whole countryside that a smart young preacher would want except you.

"Wahl. Howard and I would be proud as all that. Why, salt, what're you going to do? They're going to leave. This's the end for them. If you made enough money here to pay your debts, what will you do? Salt and pepper on sparrow's tail. Too many people just walk to a cliff and fling themselves over the edge. It never made sense to me. Like Jeb Trace.

"I always knowed what was going to happen with a man.

130

First time I saw those laughing gray-blue eyes, I knew I saw the devil in him. He wasn't going to stay here. I told Howard, that man isn't going to stay here. I could look into his eyes and tell he was going to die. It wasn't the first time.

"Wild. But I didn't see that in you. I probably would have seen it in Sarah, but all I know about her, except for the one time I saw her, is what I've heard. All I could see in Jeb Trace was that he didn't care. I never have seen that in you."

She got up. "You can't have seen all I've seen without knowing these things. The only chance you've got is with us, Howard?"

He came in with a cut-glass beaker of silver water. Put it on the table beside her bed. "I went all the way up the mountain for that, young lady," he said. "There's a spring up there that's the purest in these parts. I'll show it to you sometime. That's water, Miss Brooks, that's really water."

"She'll be all right, Howard," Elvira said. "I'm sure she'll be all right. Haven't all three of us a right to expect happiness?"

"I think we do," said Howard. "I sincerely believe that. I think we have a God-given chance."

"I'm sure we do," said Elvira.

"We're going to leave this door wide open, young lady," said Howard, "wide open. You want anything, you just yell."

She felt her cheeks trying to expand in mockery. Her cracked lips were parted, but her tongue was sealed to the inside of her mouth.

"The poor dear might not be able to call us, Howard," said Elvira, "no matter how much she wants to. I've talked to her and I'm sure she understands. Yay-es. Why don't you moisten her mouth, Howard, I'm sure she wants you to."

Howard came forward and picked up the silvery beaker. He lifted Madi from behind. She felt very light to herself coming up.

"Young lady," said Howard, "this's the best water you've ever had in your life."

She supposed it was an animal thing. She supposed it in a calm, thinking pool far in her mind where she was idly swimming. She would have preferred her denial of the water to be an act of supreme human will. But it was probably animal. Most human beings did not beat themselves to death against the walls of cages, and most human beings did not become more and more intractable under torment; but some animals and birds did. Very well, then, she would rather be an animal.

The water flooded over her face, but she would not lick it.

"She's insane," said Elvira.

"Afraid so," said Howard. "I guess we have a real one, after all. I didn't think so, but she's proven it to us. I've heard of these cases. The only people you can't make to eat or drink are insane."

"I told you about it," said Elvira stoutly.

"Guess you did, but I've heard about it before."

"What're we going to do, Howard?"

"I don't rightly know."

"If she dies," said Elvira, "we won't get the pension."

"I know that, and that's kind of rough. We have good plans."

"She'll die pretty soon, Howard."

"I know, I've seen them others."

He stroked his chin. "I guess all we can do is get really rough. Get a funnel and make it all go down."

"It won't work, Howard."

"Why won't it?"

"When they get like this, that can kill 'em. I've seen it with the maniacs. They have convulsions. I've seen people who wanted to keep their maniacs and couldn't do it."

"Wahl, we can't just let her go off like this and then tell the colonel. He might think it's ill-treatment."

"We're going to lose our pension, Howard, but we don't want to lose the place, too."

"I'll go down and get him," said Howard, glowering over Madi. "I'll do down and get him. Why can't anything ever go right?"

Madi lay on a serrated plain. Whenever she tried to move, the bruising heat found her. She forgot to move and lay stiffly in a grave made of shrinking heat. She could feel her hands curl. Her fingers turned to her palms, her dry hair closed against her head. She was loose and taut all at once. Her flesh was flabby and her innards were tight and scorched.

It did not matter anymore. There was a faint light of fall afternoon coming into the room, but there was more than that. There was an endless plain with distant mountains, and on the plain ragged, naked people walked to a horizon that blazed with purple flame. She felt a dry rasping laughter in her, and wondered whether she was insane, as they said. It had come to her mind that in this present desert that she might inherit for all time, no squiggly things that came out of drains could exist. She had always hated them, so heaven would be better. Her lips cracked when she began to laugh.

132

"Get me water," said the voice of the colonel.

"Howard went all the way up the mountain to get that good spring water for her, sir, and she wouldn't take it."

"Get me any water," the colonel said.

Madi's hot dusty eyes were looking at him, the long blond curls and the emeralds in his face. She worked her lips and tried to work her tongue. She was hotter than ever. There was no ash in the pit of her passion. Her hatred wanted to speak.

As she tried to pull words upward and hurl them only acid came and seemed to burn deeper corrugations in her throat. Her tongue seemed to be a cinder on which she was choking. The coating on her tongue was thick in her mouth. She was in another dungeon, the dungeon of the inarticulate self. She wanted to escape. She wanted to be free, her words to be free. Her words were dry prisoners huddled against the walls of her mind and her tongue and mouth were iron doors they could not pass.

Only her eyes could burn her hatred against him; but he was not looking at her eyes. He was looking at her useless mouth, and rubbing drops of water over her lips.

"Don't drink much," he was saying, "don't drink much."

Her mouth was avid but not to drink—to speak!

He misinterpreted. "Don't be greedy, don't be greedy, a little at a time."

Her hatred was impatient. Release for her lips and tongue! Release to tell him.

He patted water on her cheeks. Her wrists and hands were immersed in water. Some drops of rolling water feeling icy were going between her breasts. He plied water softly against her hair. Water clung to her lips. Water escaped down the sides of her tongue.

Water swept down her throat. Water expanded in her heart and its dry, listless beat began to heighten. Water uncurled her fingers. The fluttering dry pulse in her wrists slipped away under the veins.

Her tongue began to live.

She felt like a corpse whose mouth was becoming alive and fierce.

"She's insane," said Elvira. "Only the insane will do that."

"Or the resolute," said the colonel.

"You know how they get, sir," said Elvira. "The ones that ain't of the flesh anymore."

"I know how they get," said the colonel.

133

"What makes them that way, sir?" asked Elvira.

"Despair, morbidity. The one is just human, the other is a mental thing." He was applying the water, slowly, cautiously, inward and outward.

"We're sorry she's insane, sir," said Howard. "We've done our best."

"Fuck you," said Madi.

A silent room.

Madi's thick tongue worked again. "As for you, Colonel," she said, "I know your brother is somewhere under the false press in the room with the treadmill. Liar, liar, liar. Who wears his hair like his brother's, who claims military victories! Who tried to ingratiate himself to his brother's wife with his poetry. Who sits as a lord above his brother's bones and tries to seduce his children. Who is protected in his ineffectiveness by a mute loyal sergeant. Immoral thief, liar, tyrant, and traitor!"

Harte Trace stood up. "Don't lock her in, there'll be no more of that nonsense. She'll do what she wants, and you'll be kind to her. She is the mistress here. Now I have no other choice but to finish a long business that has been waiting for a long time."

ᗑ∢ CHAPTER VII ⫸ᗕ

THE NIGHT WAS DARK AND THE ROOM
was warm. There was a glowing still from the fire. The new
windows that Howard had put in rattled a little in cold night
wind. He hadn't done as good a job as the person who first
put the windows in. Or had the girl who had been here in
the long ago break windows, too?

Madi, lying in bed, had been having a curious experience.
She had felt herself literally expanding, her flesh becoming
round and smooth again. It was an unsettling experience. It
made you realize how almost intangible the human body was.
It was not a solid substance like iron. It was an airy castle
of delusion. You thought you were muscular, solid, weighty,
substantial, but you could blow away on a wind if fluid did
not weigh you down. Like a balloon, you needed ballast.
The gushing stream kept your feet on the ground.

Her brain had seemed to expand also. Maybe it had. Those
tissues would need water, also. And as it expanded, the hard,
bitter kernel it had become had unfolded, and hatred was
not tight and fierce, it was wondering and afraid of what she
might have let loose in this embattled community. Not that
she regretted what she had said and done—that would be
martyrdom of a senseless kind. But now she could reflect
upon consequences in the dark and feel perturbed about
what they might be.

Some form of action was going to take place, and any
form of action that would take place in this situation would
be one that would have dire results for someone. There was
no action possible here that would not culminate in tragedy.

She wondered about herself as she lay here, coolly con-
templating inevitability of tragedy. There was no scorching
fear in her mind, no prickly giant of anxiety. Was she at last
submitting to the inertia of fatalism? She hoped not. She had
learned something in the recent days—that she was passionate and that she deemed it a glorious thing. Passion was
not something she would like to push aside as a used tool or

135

as painful emotion it would be as well to be without. It could be flaming, injurious pain cupped in your hands, but it was a treasure she pitied people without it. It was treasure even if it killed you, as it had probably killed Jeb Trace and Sarah. But they were brilliant flashes of nobility to her. They had been so alive, alive. They were still. Only to be yourself without compromise was to be alive. When you compromised, you became part of someone else, of the schemes and designs of that someone else, and part of you was stolen forever and nothing was empowered to return it to you.

She lay in a cup of sleep, as in a dark valley below cliffs. Her spirit was calm, and her sleeping face reflected it. The dying fire reflected softly from her cheeks, on which the gauntness of willful deprivation still showed. The dark shadowed the hollows. There was a strong self-reliance in her face, curiously gentle. It was as if she had successfully met herself and had not needed to turn away in shame or self-deceit. The person she had sought for a long time was adequate, and she slept in the tranquillity of the relief few people have the opportunity to find.

She had thought about how insubstantial the human body was, made always literally of the fragile compounds of air and water. She had not thought about the spirit that had made it possible to accept this and fall asleep in peace. Her dreams might not have told her that the spirit had proven that it was not merely made of air and water and that it could deny sustenance for that fragile body if it chose. But the dying heat on her glowing face showed firm lids and placid lips and a straight body under the covers. Her power was resting without fear.

Full light was in the room when she awoke. She awoke placidly, conscious that someone had entered the room. A subdued Elvira was in the doorway with a tray. "Ham and eggs, biscuits and coffee," she said.

Madi sat up and plumped the pillow behind her. Her hunger was a wild child, but she would not let anyone see it. It had poise. A gift from its mother.

"I can't think of anything nicer," Madi said, pleasantly.

Elvira blinked. Where was the virago? She brought the tray forward eagerly. "Did you want to eat alone or shall we visit?"

"Why don't you get a cup of coffee and we'll visit?" said Madi.

While Elvira was gone, Madi sniffed the aroma of the

breakfast. It was her first breakfast, even if she was not yet aware of it. She knew she was one of the quick and that the dead were not eating this morning. But she did not fathom her ability to sit before the breakfast, with all animal instinct mounting in her, and yet wait patiently for Elvira to return.

Elvira came hurrying back in rather a stumbling haste that Madi found amusing, but she concealed it. Elvira had spilled coffee into her saucer.

"Where's Howard?" asked Madi, putting fork and knife into a pungent piece of ham.

"Ice fishin'. Yay-es. That man can just take his ax and pole and pocket sandwich and blanket and go off there to his little shack with the wheels on it and sit out there all day. I always wonder what he thinks about."

"Perhaps he's wise in some ways," Madi said.

"I suppose so," said Elvira resignedly. "My stomach rumbles something terrible in the night, but I don't believe I've ever heard a rumble out of Howard."

"These biscuits are delicious."

"I believe I was baking biscuits by the time I was nine years old. Yay-es. In those days girls learned early. It isn't that way now. You couldn't get yourself a little helper these days."

"What's on the eggs?"

"I make a little batter. I stiffen the eggs up a little and then I pour the batter in the pan. It hardens around them right away and leaves 'em soft but with the white pretty well cooked, and the yolks able to pour so you can mop your meat. I use some wheat flour in milk, with some melted Vermont cheddar. Howard goes over there to the cheese mill once in a while. Then a few seeds, some salt and pepper. It makes it real tasty."

"It certainly does," said Madi.

"I've always prided myself," said Elvira. "You have to feel something about the things you do. I don't think anybody can pickle better than I do. It sounds easy to pickle things, but it isn't. Yay-es. People that don't know think it's easy to make coffee. But it's the simplest things that are always the hardest. They think it's only some coffee and water and make it hot. It isn't that way. I put some egg shell in mine. Clears it. Makes it sharper. Guess that's the only word. The shells off your very eggs went into the coffee."

Madi sipped the coffee. "Wonderful."

Wasn't everything?

She had made a return to a place where she had never been but which she had been born for. It was nice to be home and everything was savory. She had worked back into her original skin, and it was comfortable on her. She would have worn it comfortably before if she had known it was there. But circumstances had never allowed her to find Madi. Before that was possible, she had been bewildered by her father, although he was understandable enough. He was an improvident drunk. That in itself did not bewilder her: what had bewildered her was how could a daughter of an improvident drunk be what she would have liked to have been? The specter of her father was always in the skin, and in her mirror she had seen his eyebrows, coloring, and hair—and what else could be lurking to defile her?

And she had been bewildered by her mother, although she had stoically walked by her side through it all. Now she knew, without thinking about it, that her mother had had only one thought in mind, that the women in the family should take the mop—and was that not woman's duty?—and clean the house behind the dirt from the man's shoes.

She knew that, but she did not know that she was not going to think about it. What she was going to like to remember was her mother's bravery as she was dying, and the sentimental thought of the coffin spinning down into the green deeps of the sea past the eyes of fish rather than neighbors who would have said, "Poor Mrs. Brooks," with the joy in their eyes of the equally deprived.

She wasn't going to think about what she really thought about, and that was that her mother had been goddamn presumptuous to think that the daughter owed Mr. Brooks anything.

"You don't mind if I tip my saucer into the cup, do you?" said Elvira.

"Don't be silly. Do you cure this ham?"

"No, we used to do our own, but Mrs. Fletcher, a widow outside the village on the East—she's famous for cobblers, she has a formula. You can't really beat that woman. She's all bent over, just looks like a withered stick. But you can't beat her. She has a daughter who isn't quite right. Her eyes swim around in her head, but she can help out Mrs. Fletcher real good. The only thing everybody worries about is what's to become of the girl when Mrs. Fletcher's gone. Howard just shrugs when that's talked about. He says people like Mrs. Fletcher look all their lives as if they're dying but never perform the duty. He says they're too stubborn. He says the girl will flicker out like a light and Mrs. Fletcher will put flowers on the graves of all of us."

"There're people like that," said Madi.

Elvira went out to the kitchen and got more coffee for both of them, and they sat in companionable silence. Their thoughts were engraved in a different manner, but the subject of them was the same.

Elvira sipped huskily on her coffee; her throat was taut. "If Colonel's the one that gets killed," she said, "I suppose Howard and me have to look for another place to live. Halsey and that southern belle with her nose in the air or on the grindstone'd never believe we didn't know anything about it."

Elvira assumed that Madi would know what was going to happen, and her assumption was correct. Colonel Harte Trace had had no choice. He had discovered that Madi knew, and he was not able to allow her to be a prisoner. Plus she had impugned his honor. He could not keep her locked in, and therefore she would be able to tell if she wished, and he could not harbor her opinion of him, no matter how true it might be. The colonel had found himself trapped, and he would have gone back to the prison mansion and would have told Halsey and Sarah Bruce where to look.

"Did you know where they were, Elvira?"

"Yay-es. How could you not know? Jenkins making that cistern cover look like something else. But when it was all over, when all the boys left here, we thought it would be all right. Jenkins didn't make that cistern cover look like a press until after the party and all the boys had gone home. If he had, some of 'em would of known. But they all thought Jeb Trace and the others had gotten away. I guess they still believe it. Sarah Bruce and Halsey have left no stone unturned. They've seen lots of those boys.

"The party was something. Colonel still had some southern feelings. He had all through the war, I guess. He told me that when the boys were to be released to go home, there should be the best party we could make.

"Maybe he felt guilty, too. He was very sad that night when all the merrymaking was going on, A drink in his hand but not drinking it. Watching the boys. Laughing with 'em if they happened to look his way.

"I guess he wished his brother was one of them."

"Why would he wish that," said Madi, "if everybody thinks he killed his brother?"

Elvira was outraged. "Why, nobody thinks he took his own hands and killed his brother."

Madi remembered the proving fingers at her throat. "What do they think, then?"

"Why, we think, Howard and me, and from what I hear, Halsey and Sarah Bruce, that Colonel let his brother die. He was jealous of him, from what you hear. Imitated him in lots of ways. Colonel was the younger brother, and imitating ain't unusual. You see it all the time.

"But to imitate somebody you have to love him, don't you, or at least admire him. But you'd hate, too, wouldn't you? If I admire you and I imitate you, that don't mean I wouldn't like to hurt you!"

Elvira's too-candid vehemence came out of her mouth before she thought well enough about it. She paused, and her face blistered with embarrassment. Then she said hastily, "Anyway, if you admire somebody and hurt him, you can regret it, and Colonel was awfully sad that night. It was a good party, and the colonel complimented me. Yay-es. He brought me into the office. Wahl, Jenkins came and brought me there.

"The colonel stood up. I can never forget it. He told me that even in the old days in the South he had never seen a better party. I could tell he meant it. It just squeezed my heart. And my heart had been squeezed the night before. No matter what you think of me, don't think I didn't do my job. I did for those boys. I did what I could. There was more than one that kissed me good-bye, I can tell you.

"Colonel said he understood it was my home here. He said you could buy federal prisons if you wanted to, and he was going to buy this one. It couldn't be used around here for anything. Prisons are used for contract labor, but who would give a contract way out here? So the colonel wasn't going to use it for that. He just wanted it, I guess, as the tomb of his brother. That's the way the colonel is, and you can't get away from it, no matter how he seems."

What he seemed like to Madi was someone who hadn't wanted anyone to be ferreting around in the prison.

"Colonel told us we could stay here, caretake. We could've done well with it, there's a lot of land, there's a sawmill on the other side of the ridge, we could've made something maybe with the grist mill, if we could have put an engine in it. But you know Howard.

140

"Yay-es. But we were happy here. I have my garden. Howard has been hunting and fishing. He was doing some odd jobs in town. But if the colonel is the one that gets killed . . ."

Madi asked softly, "If the colonel wanted such a fine party for the men when they were released, why did he keep them in such terrible conditions here?"

Elvira had been brooding, and the question took a moment to penetrate, and then she looked up with surprised eyes.

Her voice was hushed with memory as she said, "Why, this prison was made for two hundred people. There were three thousand in here. For some reason somebody in Boston insisted there were fifteen hundred prisoners. There wasn't enough food. Colonel with his own money bought rifles and seeds. He got up in front of the men and offered to take the word of any man who would go out and hunt or make a garden. No man that he took the word from ever ran away."

"What did Jeb think of all that?"

"Jeb Trace?" Elvira's face softened. "You don't think that Jeb Trace would do anything but laugh and, when the trusted hunters brought in the meat, scorn it and eat gruel. You should of met Jeb Trace."

Madi thought that in a way she had.

It turned out that Howard hadn't gone ice fishing. While the women were drinking coffee and gathering their wits and energy for a crisis, Howard had done some fishing in the bleak walls of the prison. Perhaps he had become adept at it during the war—it would have been easy work—and he came back to the cottage with information.

He stood in the doorway of Madi's room. Elvira saw him standing there and leaped to her feet. "What're you doing standing there like that without so much as a by your leave? Don't you know this's a lady's bedroom, and she's in bed?"

"I forgot everything was changed," said Howard, drawing back.

"I thought you went fishing," said Elvira. "Why did you sneak in here like that?"

"If you couldn't hear my big feet, then you were running away at the mouth so fast thunder wouldn't of bothered you. If a horse could run like your mouth, we'd be rich."

"What've you been doing?" Elvira asked avidly, winking at Madi.

"What do you think I've been doing? I got curious about

141

the kind of fishin' they was doin' over there! So I went over. Any crime in that?"

"Can Howard come in, Miss Brooks?" asked Elvira, with a panting look.

"I'm sure he needn't stand on ceremony," said Madi. What clowns these were. Punch and Judy clowns, hilarious with clubs.

Howard came archly into the doorway. Elvira demanded, "What're they doing over there?"

Howard leaned against the doorjamb. "Wahl, Colonel told them the whole thing. Jeb and the others, ten of 'em, got into the mill when the door wasn't locked. They was waitin' for the chance. You know how Jeb Trace was always watching for a chance."

Elvira sighed. "Yay-es."

"They found it," Howard said proudly. "They sure did. Wahl, they went in there and took off the cistern cover, slid down there into the water, and tried to find their way out." He paused dramatically, smiling teasingly at Elvira. He didn't include Madi in the suspense he was building, and she could tell that he didn't care about her at all. He was playing with his wife, and Madi did not matter. He would use the proper attitude toward her, that demanded by the situation, but other than that she didn't exist.

It gave Madi a little pang to see that their world belonged to them alone. She was excluded as usual.

"Howard," said Elvira, "if you stand there and keep trying to torment me, I'm going to get very angry. I'm going to get so angry you've never seen the like before." Her face was purpling not with anger, but with lust for knowledge.

Madi watched the game they were playing with each other, but it did not move or excite her, except for her chagrin at her exclusion. Howard had brought obvious news, as evidenced by his self-satisfaction, and Elvira also knew what the news was. But she was a rustic gossip and wanted the delicious detail.

She doubtless also wanted to be tantalized, and Howard was an expert at it. These two were surely wedded in desolate country titillation.

"Did Halsey challenge him to a duel?"

"Yer gettin' ahead of yourself," he said smugly.

"What'd Halsey and her supreme highness do when the colonel told 'em?"

"I don't know. How would I know?"

"Wahl, didn't you find out?"

142

"From who? Jenkins? Who can find out anything from him? Them niggers? All I know is when I went over there this morning they was all white-faced and about as talkative as Jenkins. That's all I know."

"Then, how do you know what happened?"

"By watchin'! How else would I know?"

"Did they mind if you watched?" asked Elvira.

"They didn't seem to be minding anything. They didn't even look at me. For a minute I thought I might help Halsey, but I didn't."

"Help him do what?"

"Go down in there! What else would I help him do? Duel?"

"Why didn't you help him?"

"First place, I didn't want to go down there anyway. And it isn't my business. And he and her highness didn't look as if they wanted any help. They didn't look as if you could walk up to them and say anything. If I ever saw faces like chilled fish."

"Salt!" exclaimed Elvira.

"You put it on, then," he said, grinning. "You can't expect me to."

"Who else was there?" she asked.

"Everybody. The Colonel. Jenkins. The gray nigger."

"Where were the children?"

"Afterwards," said Howard, "the colonel called me to his office and said he wanted the children over here tonight. From supper on. We're supposed to keep them occupied."

"They're going to fight?"

"Aren't you getting ahead of yourself?" Howard asked.

"Were the children there when Halsey went down in there?"

"No, no," said Howard, "they wouldn't do that. They were with the other niggers over in the garrison."

"What did her highness do all this time?"

"Stood there," said Howard.

"Is that all she did?"

"Wahl, she stood there as if she was in a stage play. Hands around her throat, staring at heaven."

"You never saw a stage play."

"What'd you mean, I never did? Didn't those players come from Boston and give a performance for the boys? Don't you remember that woman who was always ranting and clutching at herself with her eyes staring?"

"Did her highness fall on the floor like the other one?"

"No, she didn't," said Howard judicially. "I saw her about

143

to fall a few times. If she had, she would've gone right down into the cistern. She swayed right on the rim there a few times, but I thought the colonel could probably catch her. He was right there holding the lantern down there on a rope for Halsey. Halsey was splashing around down there."

"Did she almost fall in?"

"She threw her arms around a few times, and one foot was right against the curbing. The colonel was holding the rope and looking down in there, and I don't think he saw it. But I wasn't going to go over there. With the look on her face and the way her arms whirled around, I was afraid she'd take me down with her."

"She was suffering," said Elvira.

"If I clutched my throat that way," said Howard, "I'd suffer, too."

There was a long, definite pause. These two veteran gossips knew when to halt for the denouement. Both of them knew what it would be, just as Madi knew, and had known since she saw Howard's grinning face in the doorway. But they wanted to lick the meat before they ate it.

"I don't suppose Halsey found anything," said Elvira cautiously, looking at Howard with a worried frown.

He did not let her down. "There's a lot of water down there," he said. "There was quite a splash when Halsey went down in."

"He could have been killed," said Elvira.

"He wasn't."

"How long did it go on?" Elvira asked.

"About two hours, I suppose."

"What was the colonel doing all this time?"

"Swinging the light around so Halsey could see what he was doing."

"Did you go over there and look in?"

"I don't look into the devil's face if I can help it."

Elvira looked at her worn hands. They mystified her for a while as she turned them here and there, as if to certify them as her own.

"What did he come up with?" Her eyes stayed on her hands now quietly folded in her lap.

"Few bones. One was sort of like a leg bone, I imagine. Couldn't tell from where I was standing, but it looked gnawed."

"Did her highness faint?"

"Naw. She held onto her throat. If her throat was longer, she would of climbed it."

"Jeb Trace's bones?"

"Now, who could know that?" demanded Howard. "I ask you, woman, who could tell that?"

"Then, they're not going to fight?" asked Elvira plaintively, disappointedly.

"What made you get that idea? Not going to fight? The cistern was concealed, wasn't it? Bones were in there, weren't they? They want us to take the children tonight and until further notice, don't they?"

Elvira's hands were big and helpless in her lap. "If Colonel is the one that gets——"

"I've thought of that," shouted Howard, "I've thought of that. Do you think I haven't? I'm going fishin'." He whirled and went out and the door of the house slammed.

"They can't duel, can they?" asked Madi. "In the West, but not here."

Elvira slowly lifted her head and looked at Madi pointedly. "There's only one that would tell," she said.

Madi shook her head. "No, there isn't," she said. "No."

⚔ CHAPTER VIII ⚔

LOOKING OUT THE OPEN FRONT DOOR
in late afternoon, Madi, with a heavy shawl around her, saw
Elvira and Howard bringing the children from the prison
mansion. Howard was pulling the three children on a sled,
and Elvira was cavorting around and pelting them all, including Howard, with handfuls of snow. And then her soft,
bundled bulk collapsed in the snow. Howard stopped pulling,
put his hands on his hips, and laughed at her. She was
sitting spraddled in the snow, and kept lifting her head up
and down with hopeless laughter. The children tumbled off
the sled and pelted her with snow. Finally Howard got Elvira
on the sled and he and the children helped each other pulling
her up the slope.

It had been a scene of distinct human mystery. It had been
pretty, with no right at all to it.

Madi was not ready to greet them on those terms. With a
stealth she did not understand, she closed the door on the
cold and the sight of them, got her coat from her room, and
slipped out the back door, keeping the shawl bundled around
her head. She walked up the back slope into the pines and,
because she was still weak, rested on an ice-encrusted rock.
A trickle of water passed over the rock and congealed stead-
ily. She sat on the granite edge. She stood up and brushed
her skirts and followed the ridge to the oversite of the burial
field where she had first seen Sarah Bruce at work. She did
not go down among the graves; it was not necessary. What
she wanted to find here was an essence, a relative plane between life and death—or was she looking for a plane of
truth? She certainly had not seen it in the pretty portrait of
laughing children and two indulgent adults coming up in the
hard snow to a warm cottage for dinner and charades?

She did not know what she wanted. To commune with
these dead spirits? They were dreams to her, as perhaps they
were to themselves or to those who had known them. For
the moment she was a dream to herself. In a way that had

always been true. Her life had always been one that floated beneath her and that she did not accept. She had never been able to hold a brick in her hand and lay it on another and say this is my house and a good one and I will be true to it as it will to me until I die.

In the cold wind, blowing easterly, she heard no portents. The wind seemed to brush memories from her cheeks. She was a figure who walked here. her part in a drama gone. She felt her shadow move offstage, before events that her hand could not stay. I hope I am not a fatalist. she thought.

Chilled. she had a sudden desire for warmth and gaiety. Let the picture be a false one. it could seem real while it was happening. The fireplace would be roaring now, with Howard probing at it. The children's eyes would be forgetting into the flames, and the promise of hot chocolate and scones would be rich on their mouths.

Wind plucked at her, and she heard a sigh of flicks of frozen snow among the graves. She lifted her eyes and the mute prison mansion had some lights below her. Cold water flowed under it where men had gone and dungeons were silent beneath it with what animal, what plant dark until light revealed its awful color? What hearts beat there this evening. who ate, who would sleep, who would tomorrow sleep forever? How many would he join here?

What deceit curled and shriveled there and knew that tomorrow it would match its tension and guilt against an enemy with truth in his weapon?

The cottage was alight with animation. Madi came in the rear door, her shawl in her hand and unbuttoning her coat. The children espied her and ran for her, hurtling. passionate, embracing. Their faces were hot and from the cheeks of one she found salt on her lips.

Everyone was cloaked in the primary characteristic. Elvira was filled with vital generous energy, bustling around and talking and no one listening and Howard laughing at her and smoking a pipe and grabbing a girl as she went by and tickling or tugging at her while she screamed with delight, and in all this the girls were prime selves, the hungry Polly Ann with scone jelly sweet and glistening on her mouth. and Marcy, the dreamer, exclaiming. "I won't be baked in the oven for Polly Ann, I'm not Gretel," and Liz, the practical one, saying, "You wouldn't make good gingerbread anyway."

Appetites were inspired during a glorious picnic. No dull sitting around a table and knowing what was there. All was magic. Now a sausage from the kitchen. There were two kinds. Elvira would hold a smoking sausage of one kind behind her back in a napkin and another in the same way in the other hand.

"I've got a kiss for the one that gets the venison sausage!" said Howard.

"I don't want the venison one!" said Marcy, pointing at one of Elvira's arms.

"You got the venison!" cried Elvira. "Get her, Howard!"

"Don't think I won't."

Screams.

The fire danced in a more majestic way. It had become an adult fire, no matter how much Howard with a less swift arm probed music into it.

The treasures from the kitchen were no longer treasures because no one was hungry.

No one could see how solemn the night might be outside, because the windows were enigmas against the hot, lighted room. Eyelids began to fall. Elvira said, "Shall we play a game?" and even Howard did not answer.

The fire spoke to itself, erratic and answering any way that anyone wanted. Madi thought she heard the ticking of a clock. She looked around and did not see any clock. It came to mind that she had not seen a clock since she had been in this place.

Liz, the practical one, yawned, and said, "I guess they found Daddy after all."

ᴏᴥᴀ(CHAPTER IX)ᴥᴏ

POLLY ANN, THE HUNGRY ONE, WAS sleeping with Madi, and she was hungry even in sleep, hungry for warmth and the feeling of another body close. At first, in her sleeplessness, Madi had found the clinging of the child a respondent to a hunger she had herself, but after a while she began to sweat and itch in the contact. The covers were deep and Howard had replenished the fire before they had all retired. Madi wanted to pull away from the child but would not abandon her. It was laughable to allow a little thing like some stinging sweat disturb the girl's sleep. And, after a while, it was pleasant to have the girl cuddled close to her as the fire dimmed and died in the night and only eyes were left in it and cold slipped up through the bed from the floor, and cold began to remember her in her mind and bestir itself. Then she began to hold the child close to her, as if she were holding herself and perhaps in a way she was.

She sensed the clockless coming of morning. It awakened in her with a dull pain. She could remember an old man in the jail who was always clutching his abdomen and describing to anyone who would listen how dull the knife was that was turning in there. He had seemed to wish that the knife was sharper, and therefore, in some way, more promising. More promising of what? Madi had smiled about it then, as best she could. But now she understood. The dull pain told you that you might have to wait a long time, and the sharp pain told you that soon it would be over.

She did not know what had been wrong with the old man, and she could not tell what was wrong with her. It was proper that she should feel pain, because so much depended on what would happen today. But neither the dullness of the pain nor the thoughts in her mind could explain to her what she wanted to happen—if she wanted anything at all to.

What could she want to happen? She loved no one, not even herself. She had more respect for herself than she had

149

had before, but that was nothing like love. It just made love for someone else more possible. But there was no someone else. The reason why it made love for someone else more possible was that you thought you had something to offer. How could you love someone with nothing to give for it?

You could only dare love if you knew you had resources that would as far as possible help or protect your lover. A weak woman would turn her love over to the police, the lion —or the creditor. Her mother must have been strong. She had not abandoned her husband even after he was dead. She had continued to fight for him in the debtors' jail, with ten thousand revolutions of the hand mill a day in her gnarled, helpless hands. Yes, her mother had had that, it was true, but that had been a bit too much. That had been like Sarah Bruce, a romance, carried too far into distance. A romance, a dream. Die for your love but not at the sacrifice of the products of it. Don't make the children drown in the dream with you.

She knew now why when she cradled Polly Ann she was cradling herself.

The sense of morning was tightening around her; it was a garment she was to wear this morning. She did not have to put it on; it had been slipping up her feet and over her throughout the night. Looking back over her forehead and her hair and the ridge of the hair of the child against her, she saw grayness. She had seen it earlier but had known it was not the gray of real dawn. It had been a gray that waited to make her feel sensitive to the true morning that was hesitating. Hesitating? It was not now. She felt wings on its haste. She felt like a laborer who was waking to go down into the mines and he had been told in advance that today the shaft would collapse. Yet there was no possible way in which he could avoid going to the job.

There was no possible way in which she could avoid going to the job. And her job was to watch someone get hurt or killed. The great slumbering pain in her that was beginning to stretch or burn and kick made her think in a horrible way about childbirth. She was imagining a woman who had been raped by a man who might have been infected or who was a beast in his mind. And the woman was in pain and waiting to see what she would find.

It would be a great deal easier for Sarah Bruce this morning. An odd thing to think. She, Madi, was not important here; it was of no more concern to her than it was to Elvira and Howard. To Madi, as to Elvira and Howard, it was bread and butter. To Sarah Bruce it was the culmination of a quest she would not abandon; it was vengeance. She had the bones of her husband, if only in symbol, and she had a gallant who would fight for her and the denial of her romance.

So how could she, Madi, think that this approaching morning was easier for Sarah Bruce than for her? It was simple enough: Madi did not believe that the outcome of the duel was for her a simple matter of comfort, or lack of it, as it appeared to be for Elvira and Howard. In some manner her involvement was far more profound than that.

She belonged here, to this. She had suffered for it by suffering for herself. Sarah the ghost and Jeb Trace were gossip to Elvira and Howard, but Sarah and Jeb Trace were the spirit of Madi Brooks.

It was easier for Sarah Bruce this morning because she knew which man was the one who should be killed. All she had to worry about was whether it would happen as it must if God was just.

Madi was not sure. She was sure when she was being imprisoned and tortured by Elvira and Howard, but she was no longer sure when Harte Trace released her and told Halsey and Sarah Bruce about the false mill press. He might have felt forced to tell them in order to protect some portion of his honor. realizing that probably Madi, released. would tell them. On the other hand. it had not been necessary for him to release her. But could he have some weakness in him, some strange weakness that would allow him to put a false cap over his brother's tomb and be unable to keep Madi a prisoner. be unable to retain command in a battlefield when he had to hold wounded Sergeant Jenkins in his lap?

Everyone said he would not be able to kill his brother, or anyone, or almost anything else. for that matter. by his own hand. And yet everyone, including those most beholden to him. Elvira and Howard, thought he had killed his brother. How? By allowing him to think he could escape through the cistern. knowing he couldn't, and then refitting the cap so the men could not return by the way they had left?

This would be the way of the world's worst coward. A man who could not stand the sight of pain or blood but who could go and write his poetry and read a book when men in the caverns below him were finding their throes.

But he had strangled her, Madi, leaping around the table like a cat, catching her so fast she had no time to move, putting her close to death with little effort. But wasn't that easy for a trained soldier? Didn't he know how far he could go without really harming her? Of course he would know. Could he really kill? He had known he was not going to hurt or kill her. He was trying to disprove something others said about him, but it was no proof at all.

It terrified her to realize that she was in the same position as Sarah Bruce, or somewhat the same position. Madi had been trying to tell herself that she had no way of knowing or caring which man should live. Her thinking as the dawn approached had showed her that this was not so. Nowhere in her thinking had Halsey appeared, except as the faintly perceptible opponent. All her rationalization had been about Harte Trace.

She was his champion, whether he deserved it or not.

Her position was worse than Sarah Bruce's! Sarah Bruce believed in Halsey and his mission. Madi could only hope to believe in Harte Trace.

And if everything that was said about Harte Trace were true, he would die this morning. His remnant of southern honor would make him stand there, but he would take Halsey's bullet like a fool.

She slid from the entangled girl and, shivering, dressed. She slid from the room and found Elvira standing in nightgown and robe in lamplight turned low. The room was shrunken in the dim light, and Elvira was crawled down into her robe, which was blue with some piping that light reflected from.

Elvira whispered, "We have to talk low so we won't wake Howard. He worked hard last night tryin' to make everybody happy. And we shouldn't wake the children. I guess he got them right tired out, even little Marcy. She's the one I was worried about. She thinks too much."

She pointed to a table. "I knew you'd be out here, so I got coffee ready. It's still steamin' some."

"I don't think I could."

"You won't miss anything," said Elvira. "I've been watchin'. The lights just went on in the garrison. They'll be having breakfast there soon. Duels are always in real light, never otherwise."

Madi was shocked that she wanted coffee. At a time like this you should be more austere. She gulped at the coffee.

"What do you know about duels, Elvira?"

"What do I know about duels? Why, most everything.

152

With all the southern gentlemen that was in here, I heard a lot."

"Will they walk toward each other and shoot?" asked Madi.

She did not like the excitement tingling through her; it was as indecent as wanting the coffee so much.

"Wahl, no, I don't expect so," said Elvira. "I've heard about that, it's in the papers and a magazine we get. And those thrillers Howard reads, if I don't find 'em first and put them in the fire. No, I don't think so. Colonel and Halsey ain't been out in the West. No, I expect it'll be old-fashioned code duello." She spoke the words with maternal pride. As if they had come from her loins, or should have.

"And what happens?" asked Madi. She was glad that the one big animal gulp of the coffee had been enough, and that anxiety had replaced animal excitement. Now she did not want to go from gossip and thrill; she wanted to know the way the danger stood itself and commanded the ground.

Deliciously Elvira said, "I expect it'll be sabers or dueling pistols. They're both cavalry, so it might be sabers. That'd mean a lot of blood." She shuddered ecstatically.

"What're you women doing out here?" Howard asked, coming in from the bedroom. He pointed to the loft. "Do you want to wake the kiddies, is that what you want to do?"

"Madi's going over there," said Elvira, "so I thought I ought to tell her something about dueling."

"There's no sense talking about it," said Howard. "All she needs to know is that these are two rebels and they don't give a damn!"

"Keep your voice down," said Elvira.

"They're out to kill each other, and one is going to do it."

"Which one?" said Madi.

"I guess Halsey kills easiest," said Howard. "Colonel might remember something, but he might remember it too late. Anyway, the colonel would just as soon not kill Halsey, but Halsey would just as soon kill the colonel."

"Will that make a difference?" asked Madi.

"If you're going to stick somebody or shoot a gun," said Howard, "it matters a lot whether you want to or not."

"Are you sure," asked Madi, "that Colonel Trace wouldn't want to kill anyone in a stand-up fight?"

"Listen, Madelaine," said Howard, forgetting the *Miss Brooks*, "you're in the same position we are. If Colonel is killed, it probably won't be so good. Those people think we're all on his side. But I don't want to lose any sleep over it. It won't do any good. You don't think, do you, that they'd take any fightin', killing cavalry officer who could fight Morgan to a standstill, like Colonel says he did, and put him in a place like this, do you? With the war only half over? A place like this that Elvira could run? For this they're going to take out of the field a man who could beat Morgan?"

"Lower your voice, Howard."

"Sorry. I guess I'm a little bothered. I hear one of the little girls up there, Viry."

"Why didn't you keep your voice down?" She went toward the loft stair.

Howard did not pay any attention to Elvira. He took one of Madi's hands and patted it. "I know how you feel," he said, "and so does Elvira. Like us, you could have depended a lot on this. Take my advice and don't go to see it." He smiled and patted her hand coaxingly. "Go on back to bed," he said. "You'd be surprised how things pass over. Elvira and I have found that out many times. Anyway, why not look on the bright side of things? Her highness down there might want you to keep charge of the children, she might want us to. We all might be here and keeping things going. You have to look on the bright side."

She did not have any contempt for him. He was beyond the place where it could have any value. She was not even repulsed by the touch of his hand. In the world he lived in, he was being kind to her.

"If you've got to go," he said, "we'll make it all right. You don't have the strength Elvira and I do. You never had hope for comfort before, but we've always known you can have it if you hope and try hard enough. So we're not afraid. But you go if you want. We've got some things for you."

He took her by the hand, and she allowed it. He gave her a lamp and heavy gloves, inspected her boots and pronounced them all right, and put a sandwich in her pocket.

"It's roast beef," he said, "and rye bread. One week Viry bakes it with seeds and the next she don't. I like it best with the seeds and always ask her why she don't bake it that way every week? She always says you need a change. I ask her why. She says you need a change. What can you do with a woman like that?" He looked over her shoulder. "They're getting up down there. It'll be getting light soon, but take my advice and use the lantern. This's rough ground here and there." He closed the door.

They were getting up down there. She saw smoke from two chimneys, and lights in the garrison quarters. It would not have been possible from here to see lights in Colonel Trace's rooms at the northwest side of the prison. But Harte Trace was up. One of the smoking chimneys was from the northwest side. Or was Jenkins making fire and the colonel was asleep? No, the colonel would not be asleep unless he had drunk too much. Why would he drink too much? Afraid? She did not think he would be afraid. If he was afraid, it would be fear of killing someone else, not fear of being killed himself.

Eastern light was behind her as she went down the snowy slope, and the snug cottage with the children was behind her, and to the south of the cottage the village of graves with the white crosses and marble markers obscured in snow. Ahead of her rose the fifteen-foot stone wall, with the top beginning to glisten as the light struck the sharp glass and metal. Her lamp threw light over the points of her boots as if she scuffed light from the surface of the hard snow.

She was sure that she would never have known that she loved Harte Trace if she had not been walking down the hill this morning to find out whether he would die soon.

~✦(CHAPTER X)✦~

SHE DID NOT TRY ANY OF THE SIDE gates, she walked around to the front gate, through which she had originally entered when Elvira had been sitting there shelling peas. The gates were open and Madi walked in with something open in herself. Sarah Bruce would be there and now Sarah Bruce was her enemy.

She turned around quickly, as if someone had touched her on the shoulder. A blaze was beginning in the east. The person who had touched her on the shoulder was the memory of herself as she had first entered here. The memory was so vague it was filmy. She hadn't been real when she entered this unreal place: she was real now, and the place was real. Anything bizarre about it was not present this morning. Life and death were present. They always had been here but not with the sharp force of this dawn. Nothing of life and death in her past had been focused, had been blazing as the rise of this morning's sun. The death of her father had been an erasure; the death of her mother had been a dream long in coming and a nightmare in retrospect. She had never experienced death that could come in an instant from the sharp report of a pistol or the swing or thrust of a saber. Death she had known before had always been of the anticipated kind. She had gotten used to the death of her mother far before it had happened. She could not get used to the possible death here this morning because it was an enigma. And because her emotions were not calloused. And because she was not a fatalist, after all. In jail it could be recommended that one become a fatalist. You could let all the vivid scenes lower their voices and you walked asleep through the valley of it, barely allowing yourself to think about a doorway at some ending through which you could walk into a life of another kind.

Snowbirds were fluttering about and pecking at something on a shelf stuck from a window of the administration building. Probably Elvira had put out some suet.

The long hall past the colonel's office. The water that had been flowing down the walls in places was still doing so, freezing on the way. She wondered why the frozen clumps of water turned green. Something from the plaster on these walls, something from the place where the water lived? Why did the water still flow if it was so cold? It must be current water or water from depths below the frost line.

Her steps did not boom on this corridor floor. They would boom all too soon in the rotunda. Her light transfixed the rough columns of ice on the green walls. The corridor would be awash when all that frozen water melted. She paused at the open door before going into the rotunda.

Her light swung in her hand. Herself, or a breeze? She listened for feral feet, for the padding steps of a dog. There was nothing. She stood in the doorway to watch morning creep over the floor from the eastern windows. Shrouded deep back in there were the massive doors to the mill room, the guilt room. Had a man been baked into bread? She remembered the pocket sandwich that Howard had given her. She felt a hysterical note touch the tip of her tongue and sting her lips. Did Howard think she should eat the sandwich while watching the drama? Perhaps she should have brought her knitting.

The paving of the rotunda was revealing itself; the distant groined ceiling was dark except for light slipping through some chinks in the parting dome. Light was breeching the parapets of the tiers and bathing in the small tubs of the worn stairs like nebulous birds. Faint sounds rustled like flying skirts. Air drifted over the stones. The silence had breath. The cold wrapped itself for warmth around her feet and stole her own.

The damnable body did not understand austerity and portent. Her stomach gurgled and she found herself taking the sandwich from her pocket. She peered into shadows to see if anyone was watching, shielding the sandwich against her. She put down her light to one side and ravenously ate.

Dawn was a mixed marriage in the rotunda. Three Negro women came—one starkly old and gray of face and hair, leading two others, young and crinkly-haired, who were carrying a table between them. The old woman held two sabers under her left arm and a case under her right. The women wore headdresses of blue, yellow, and red. Their long skirts soughed around straight, swift legs. They made soft, quick steps over the wide floor. The two younger women placed the table in the center of the left wall between two great, barred windows. Without a clatter the gray Negress put the sabers side by side on the table and the black case beside them. The two younger women withdrew to the wall, and the gray old woman stood straight, feet together beside the table.

Madi did not know whether they had seen her. If they had, they had paid no attention. She became conscious of her light still glittering beside her feet. For some unaccountable reason she did not want it sitting there alight, and she did not want to bend down and pick it up and extinguish it and put it aside. The light was improper now. Could it distract someone, the one who was fighting while he faced this way? That was possible, just as she herself standing here might become a distraction. But she did not know where to put herself and she did not want to bend down and pluck up the light any more than you'd want to pick up a fallen handkerchief in the church aisle when the ceremony was beginning. You ignored the handkerchief and you stood in front of the lamp and kicked it back into the hallway, and she did.

Thrum, thrum, thrum on the paving, no silent graceful feet this time. Jenkins was marching in from the same corridor the women had taken. He was not in uniform, she was happy to see. But he was stiff and military and well tuckered. His boots gleamed and his mute throat was embraced by a collar and a black tie. His trousers were over his boots and he wore a gray huntsmen's tunic but no overcoat.

With military precision he marched to a place directly opposite the three women and the table. Facing the wall stiffly, he did an about-face, his heels ringing. He was still a moment, then straddled his legs and clasped his hands behind him.

The groined ceiling of the rotunda was silver and gray.

As Sarah Bruce walked across the floor to join the three Negro women and the table a slant of light burned on her red hair. She was wearing boots and a black riding costume with a silver scarf at her neck. She stood on the opposite side of the table from the gray Negress, her boots firmly planted a foot apart, her hands with gripped fingers hanging by her sides. She was staring across at the stairs and the dark iron doors of the cells.

No spectator I. Madi unbuttoned her coat, let it slip to the floor, kicked it back into the corridor, and let her shoes ring as she went and aligned herself beside Jenkins, facing Sarah Bruce Trace.

158

As her eyes locked with the malign gaze of Sarah Bruce, Madi felt a shock of recognition. Not of recognition of the woman, but of a place in life. She had taken a position, and it was her first powerful stance that held more than her stance for herself. She had adopted a meaning, a cause, right or wrong, and this was her country, and that over there was theirs!

She heard high-slapping laughter. Confusing, this. Laughter as if over a dirty joke. She and her mother had heard such laughter in a terrible small hotel one evening in the lobby.

She looked at the ceiling as she had then. Male laughter could sometimes make you think of outhouses and dogs rampant in a garden in the spring when you were trying to drink tea.

It would have been nice if the ceiling had held a lyric, one of the birds could have flown across it. But the only thing up there were massive groins. Her laughter almost flew from her mouth before she could clamp her teeth over it and kill it. She sucked it in and swallowed it whole.

Did she feel Jenkins slightly turn his head toward her? She didn't know, but she did know that Sarah Bruce's eyes were twin furnaces whose doors had been opened.

Madi knew that she wasn't being frivolous; she was being aware of the fact that a man was a man, and that she had consigned herself to whatever it implied. Groins and dirty jokes were going to be important to her, or looking at a coffin was going to be important to her. Whichever way it was, she was committed as much as was the woman across the paving, whose eyes hated her. So be it. The more you hate me, the more I want your brother dead. For that matter, you don't even need to bother to hate me. I have enough without it.

The men ambled in together, in boots, breeches, and soft shirts. Madi wondered if she were the only one who would like some blankets. The men's shirts were open at the throat. They talked and laughed together but did not look around at anyone else.

Their boots echoed on the floor as they went leisurely to the table.

"You can't tell me, Harte, that that was a wild turkey. Damn it, I saw the legs on it. You went out and shot some turkey in somebody's park."

"I swear to God, Halsey, this thing was running in a pack of them and I had to ride hard to kill the damn thing."

159

"If you had to ride hard to kill that, you must've been on a rocking horse."

"It was tough when you ate it, wasn't it?"

"It was the most tender turkey I ever ate, Harte!"

"Why did your mother break her tooth?"

"That was jelly with the pits still in it! My mother was always entrusting some little girl with a pregnant duty."

They laughed and slapped their thighs.

"She did get pregnant, that little girl," said Harte. "Swallowed a watermelon."

"Might as well have."

They slapped their thighs. When they got to the table, Halsey unsheathed the sabers.

"I see you got the kind that don't work so well," said Harte, examining one of the swords.

"They worked all right for us," Halsey said angrily.

"These swinging sabers aren't any good," said Harte. "You swing at a man and cut him and then he kills you. There's too much arch in these knives. We developed the better straighter sticking saber. You stick a man and he stays sticked."

"These sabers did all right by us," said Halsey.

Harte threw down the saber with a clatter against the other.

"You don't think these are good knives?" Halsey asked.

"I told you I didn't."

"Maybe you didn't know how to use them," said Halsey. "Good cavalry knew how."

"I don't give a damn about that," said Harte. "I'm not going to argue ordnance this early in the morning."

"I give a lot of damn about it," said Halsey.

"It doesn't matter. I was challenged, so I pick the weapons. Open the case."

"Don't give me orders. You're no colonel this morning."

Sarah Bruce with a quick movement unlatched the case and stood back.

Harte Trace looked down into the case. "Those are very good looking pistols."

"They ought to be," said Halsey, "they were Granddaddy's. And those pistols have never been dishonored."

"They won't be this time either!" said Harte.

"I didn't say they would. I wouldn't let you touch them if I thought you had black hands."

The three Negro women did not wince, Madi saw.

160

"If you don't think I have black hands," asked Harte, "why do you want to fight me?"

"I can't fight a man with black hands, I'd have him whipped and killed by somebody else. But I can shoot or cut the black heart out of you."

"I'll take the pistols," said Harte Trace, moving back from the table. Halsey also moved aside. Sarah Bruce took up one of the pistols, loaded and primed it. Jenkins crossed the rotunda and loaded and primed the other.

Harte Trace lighted a cigarette, then offered one to Halsey.

"No, thanks," said Halsey. "Harte, you're wrong about the knives, just as you've been wrong about so many things."

"I wasn't wrong about the knives and I'm not wrong about many things."

"If a man can't even tell a wild from a tame turkey."

Harte drew in on his cigarette. "Do you want to make it first blood, Halsey?"

"Do you think you can satisfy me by letting me shoot your little finger off?"

"Second blood?"

"No," said Halsey.

"If a man is down," said Harte.

"If a man is down and not dead," said Halsey, "he gets his pistol again and fires when ready."

"To the death?" asked Harte.

"I guess you recognize what I'm talking about," said Halsey.

Harte threw his cigarette on the paving and ground it under his foot. "Paces?"

"Well, you're bigger than I am, so we better make it twenty instead of fifteen. In fifteen I'd have a better chance, your silhouette's that much bigger. We'll make it twenty."

"Thank you."

"You're taking this a lot calmer than I thought you would," said Halsey.

"You don't have much time to stop dreaming, Halsey," said Harte Trace. "If you don't stop dreaming in the next few minutes, you're going to be dreaming for all eternity."

"What does that mean?" asked Halsey. "What does that mean?"

"It means that I think you ought to withdraw your challenge."

"Oh, so that's what you've been aiming for? That's it? It's just as I thought, just as I thought! Goddamn, you spineless

Yankee traitor! So that's it, is it!" He gave the rebel yell and danced around the rotunda on booted booming feet. "Yayeeeee, howweee, yayeee, give me my pistol, kill him, kill him." Dancing whirling on booming booted feet in the burning light. "Hiiiiii! Hiiiii!" Whirling, turning, dancing on booming booted feet.

A spring of air moved Harte Trace's golden hair back from his calm, watching face.

The pistols were ready. They were put back into the shapes in the case and the case was closed. Jenkins took one side of the case and Sarah Bruce the other. Madi stood there and watched them cross the floor toward her, the case between Jenkins' left hand and Sarah Bruce's right. They stood in front of her.

Their hands lifted and the case was in front of Madi at waist level.

"Take the case," said Sarah Bruce. "Turn around and arrange the guns in any way you wish, return them to the case, turn around, and hand the case to us." Her voice was easy and conversational.

"Take the case?" said Madi.

Sarah Bruce's voice was contemptuous. "Take the case, move the pistols around, return the case, you fool. Sometimes one doesn't discharge, sometimes somebody has tampered. Take the case!"

Madi was shocked by the weight of it.

They stood back from her and waited. In a scornful voice Sarah Bruce said, "Turn around, you idiot. And move. You don't keep destiny waiting."

Madi turned around and opened the case. The lethal pistols were large, lovely. The barrels must have been fifteen inches long. From across the room she had not been able to see the minute workmanship. The black guns were engraved with golden leaves and vines, in intricate measure. They were works of art. Their beauty astounded her. They were machines made with such care that one could almost forget their purpose. Was this the way man made his killing weapons, as an artist, a dreamer? Dreaming of what? These guns had been made with love, and remembering what Halsey had said, that they came from his grandfather and were unsullied, she knew they had been used with love and treasured with love. To kill?

She could not touch them. They were an alien culture.

Breathtaking, savage, civilized art, incomprehensible. She had seen brutality, and none of it had been beautiful. Now she was looking into a beautiful society whose jewels could make someone as dead as despair and starvation. The guns were jewels. She moved her elbows so it would be thought that she was doing something. As she was closing the case she paused. In the handle of each weapon was a diamond. These weapons were of great value. Could it be true that Harte Trace was not supporting these people and that he was the liar?

She turned around and handed the closed case to Sarah Bruce and Jenkins. As they crossed the floor back to the table, jointly holding the box, Madi thought: I'm as you were, mother. He was a drunk and this one might be a liar and a killer, or a liar and a coward. I'm convicted as you were. A man is my prison. Thank you for the inheritance.

If he was a coward or afraid of the blood, it was getting late for him to show it.

The way he at random selected his heavy pistol and held it straight down at his side and walked to the center of the rotunda did not indicate that he was going to burst into a run or deliver a sermon on the commandment.

This latter began to bother Madi so much that she forgot that the cold was a fire working up her legs. Would this man kill his own brother-in-law? He looked so calm.

She had an urgent wish to ask him if he had eaten breakfast, if he had slept, if he had had diarrhea. He looked too impassive to be a poet.

He did not finger or look at his weapon; it was an extension of his arm. He seemed to be finding geography in the cracks in the floor. He pushed back his golden hair abstractedly. What was he thinking about? When it came time to fire, would he fire his pistol in the air as a grand gesture?

Madi hoped not. She did not think that Halsey would honor such a gesture, and the ceiling had many groins, but she had only one. That did not mean that she could claim anything from Harte Trace if he won. It meant only that her emotion for the battle was planted in his soil.

Halsey approached Harte indolently, his pistol also at trail. "Of course my mother could have broken her tooth on all the lead you had to put into that turkey to kill it."

"She didn't eat the head, did she?"

"Can you imagine my mother eating anything like that?"

"That's exactly what I mean, Halsey. I never put shot one into the good meat of that turkey."

"You're bragging a little," said Halsey.

"If truth's braggin'."

"The turkey wasn't shooting back," said Halsey.

"How did you know that?"

Halsey laughed and slapped his thigh. "Damn," he said, "I don't want this gun to go off before its time. Let me feel your back, Harte."

They went back to back.

"First warmth I've had today," said Halsey.

The rest happened so swiftly that to Madi it seemed like seconds. The men stood back to back. Obviously the second of the challenged was the one who gave the commands. Jenkins was mute, so he stamped his foot. The weapons that had been held relaxed at the end of the hand came up and the weapon arm was crooked. Jenkins beat his boot on the paving and the men took a step forward, each away from each other. Each held his pistol erect in his hand, and each held to the back of his belt with the free hand. When Jenkins had stomped twenty times, the men turned calmly, each in profile, making the smallest target, each with pistol out-pointed with a straight arm and locked elbow, each turned sideways to the other, each with the other hand held in the belt behind him.

It was an instant. The shots threw themselves in mighty leaps to the walls and to the groins above and flung themselves around there and dissolved into silence. A black hole was in the side of Halsey's head and he fell to the floor, full-length, and the floor was a broad drum under his falling.

As Harte Trace moved with swift, measured steps toward the fallen body of Halsey, Jenkins did also.

Harte leaned down and picked up the dueling pistol that had fallen on the floor from Halsey's hand. He handed it to Jenkins, along with his own. Then he turned abruptly and walked across the rotunda to the door and the corridor to his office and did not look back.

Jenkins crossed the room, placed the discharged pistols on the table beside the case and the sabers, and followed the colonel to the corridor. But he stopped in the doorway, waiting.

Madi was staring, first at the body (so quickly?) and then at Sarah Bruce and the three Negro women. They were as stiff as trees across from her. A booming step waked her and she looked to Jenkins, who was motioning to her with inclinations of his head. She turned to him and went. He preceded her, picked up her coat, and draped it around her shoulders. She heard him go back and close the door of the rotunda.

He opened the door to the colonel's office for her and she went in.

The fire in the room had obviously been made earlier and banked and the colonel was uncovering it into life. He straightened and said, "Sit down. Jenkins will bring coffee in a few minutes." She sat down on the chair beside his desk. The fire began to light upward on his hair. He was standing before the fire, his hands behind his back. "Sorry," he said, standing aside so that the fire would be direct. "You look cold."

She didn't know what she was. She had no bodily sensations, no emotions. She was a clam. She didn't even know whether she was a cold clam. She was shivering, but it seemed to be outside herself. Someone else was shivering.

"A little good warming spirit?" he asked, opening a drawer of his desk.

"No, thank you," she said, wondering if he would need a drink now. He slid the desk drawer closed and leaned his elbows on the desk, regarding her.

His eyes were steady and unhurt. She wondered if her own eyes seemed steady and unhurt. Maybe he was as stunned as she was, and the tears, the regret, whatever might come, would come later. She did not see any residue of tears or regret in his face.

"Sarah Bruce?" she asked. She wondered what Sarah Bruce could be feeling now. Stunned also? "What is going to happen to her?"

"I'm going to take her back to the plantation," he said. "She's going to dream, and that will be the best place for her to do it. I'm going to rebuild it, make it as much like it was before as possible but with modern farming and free men doing it."

"The children?" Her lips were numb and it was hard for her to make them move.

"We'll need someone," he said. "She'll be no more good for them in the future than she's been for the past few years. Do you care for them?"

She hesitated. "I don't know," she said honestly. "I haven't been able to find out. Not really find out. They are children."

"Yes, children. Therefore worthy of sympathy. I understand." He was so cold, so objective. This was the poet? The sensitive person that Sarah Bruce had cared for in a time long gone by?

"Do you wish to come with us?" he asked.

"I don't know."

Jenkins came in with coffee, served it, and withdrew. The hot liquid burned down into her and warmed her, and the fire warmed her, but it was not enough warmth.

"Perhaps you're suited to haunted things," said Harte Trace.

"Haunted?"

He nodded. "It would be a haunted life on a reconstructed plantation in Mississippi with a dreaming woman walking the halls for the rest of her life.

"But you were haunted before you came here, were you not? Have you been anything else but haunted since you arrived? Isn't being haunted your destiny?"

Yes, she had always been haunted, but she would not meekly accept that as her destiny. "I doubt very much, sir, whether I would wish to continue to work for you. It isn't because I have seen you kill. It's . . . it's because of other things."

He smiled. "The terms on which I would take you with us to Mississippi," he said, "would not be as employer and employee." His eyes did not waver. "This woman," he said, gesturing out to the rest of the place, "would crush you if you were her servant. After all, you are her enemy. Did you not stand for me at the duel?"

She stared at him. The numbness was slipping away, there was a quickening, a cold quickening, and it was more heady than the warmth. It was cold of a different kind than that inspired by lack of heat and the sound of the pistols and the dead crumbling to the floor of a man she had essentially liked, even though he was a man she could not choose, in life or death, against this one.

"I stood for you," she said coldly. His proposal had given her permission to be a woman again, as he had once before. "Do you wish me to be your wife?"

"I am asking you to be my wife."

An unbearable triumph rushed through her. She wanted to conceal it, with lowered eyes, with getting up and leaving him for a while. She had the impulse to grab something and hide behind it. She sat still and calm in front of him. I am a passionate woman, she thought with delight and shame, the knowledge coming on top of a corpse and the sorrow of another woman. I am passionate in all ways.

166

"The only reason you want me, I suppose," she said snappishly, "is because I am hardened and calloused. Your sense of loyalty to Sarah Bruce and the children forces you to take whatever you can get in the way of a wife. Just as you took whatever you could get in the way of a convict to teach in your prison."

"Your thigh seemed appetizing," he said.

Madi bridled. "Would you court a decent woman with barracks talk? Would you laugh at her and grin and lick your lips? You can think of such things a few minutes after you have killed your brother-in-law?"

He did not react to her outrage. But his voice was stone. "I killed him," he said simply, "because there was nothing else to do. I did my suffering before I killed him. I refuse to do it afterward. I mourn the wounded; I let the dead sleep. For me, as well as for themselves. I let dead people sleep, I let dead worlds sleep. I'm not going to Mississippi to dream, to regret, to slip into the past. I'm going there to take care of the wounded and to make the money to do so. If there is anything about that that you don't like, you can get up and pack your things and I'll send you off with a good packet and excellent recommendations."

Madi was not going to be put aside by his threats. Whether she took him or not, he was her man, but he was a stained man. "You," she exclaimed, "and your smooth preacher talk of taking care of people. You who are supporting all these poverty-stricken people. What about the silver plate that lay in the ground in Mississippi and was recovered?"

His green eyes were mild and filled with mirth and a remote, misty sadness. "There isn't a ruined plantation in the South," he said, "that doesn't have the silver that was planted by grandfather, or father, or the little boy, or the old nigger, or the sister that died that winter of tuberculosis. But the people that hid it only said it was under the magnolia or the chinaberry next to the garden wall or the old smithy shop. But nobody knows which magnolia." His eyes became steely. "They believe these things!"

There was a stammering in her mind. He was so placid, so sure, then so savagely sure. "Why . . . why," she faltered, "wouldn't they believe you would kill?"

"I defeated Morgan," he said. "Just as they can't believe they are poor, so they can't believe that I, of all people, was the one who defeated Morgan."

He got up and went to a file and brought out a paper and

laid it on the desk before her. She put her fingertips on the paper and read:

> Subject: Final reduction of Morgan's forces, and consequent surrender, New Lisbon, Ohio, to the command of cavalry regular forces, Colonel H. Trace, on July 26th, 1863.

> To: Commanding General, U. S. Grant.

> (1) The forces of General John Hunt Morgan have been rendered ineffective after a year of repeated attempts to defeat him by the cavalry of Colonel Harte Trace. We can consider Kentucky and Ohio now safe from Morgan's raiders.

> (2) To cover General Braxton Bragg's movement from Tullahoma to Chattanooga, Morgan began his raids into Indiana and Ohio. His forces consisted of 2,460 men. He crossed the Cumberland from Burkesville, Kentucky, July 2. On the fifth he captured the garrison at Lebanon, and on the thirteenth entered Ohio near Harrison.

> (3) Colonel Trace's regulars were close behind. Morgan marched through the suburbs of Cincinnati on the night of the thirteenth and on the eighteenth reached Portland, near Buffington Island. Battle ensued.

> (4) Morgan lost 600 men, and 600 surrendered. On the twenty-sixth, he surrendered to Colonel Harte Trace at New Lisbon. He has been consigned to imprisonment in the penitentiary at Columbus.

Madi took her fingertips from the report. The penitentiary at Columbus. As if he surmised her reaction, Harte Trace said, "He was like Jeb or, shall we say, Jeb was like him. After all, Jack Morgan was a general. Jack escaped from the prison in November. Then he went back to raising hell. Halsey was with him. We hadn't managed to capture Halsey. Jack was head of the department of Southwestern Virginia and later in the summer he took command at Jonesboro, Georgia. Halsey was his aide then. Halsey could believe I never captured Jack because Jack was active until September in sixty-four. He got himself shot in a garden in Greenville, Tennessee. They always figured that some sneaky traitor like me did it."

"Do you consider yourself a traitor?" asked Madi. She was beginning to see far into a man, but it was not far enough. She was greedy to go into him so deeply that his mind would be even more clear to her than was her own. To understand him, to understand him as if she looked into a crystal spring.

"Of course I'm a traitor," said Harte Trace. "Anybody who turns against his blood kin is a traitor. But times come when you have to be a traitor to someone. Then you have to make the choice. Are you going to be a traitor to yourself or to your heritage."

She leaned forward. She who had been beaten and scorned thought of those others who had been, and over whom this war had been fought. "The plight of the Negroes forced you to abandon the South," she said.

"The niggers? No. No, I never did care much about what happened to them. When you're brought up all your life to think they aren't human, you can get to believe it. They look different enough from us so that it's easy to believe if you grow up with it. I never gave it a thought.

"What changed me wasn't the niggers, it was the whites. Where we lived, there were some poor white people, but they weren't trash. They were only poor when you considered the difference between our plantations and the way they lived. But they were honorable craftsmen. Wheelwrights, smiths, people who made guns, operated small farms, and a few had slaves of their own.

"When I was eighteen, I took a riding trip. I found myself in country where there was a lot of trash. And these people weren't niggers. These people looked like me."

He paused and looked off at the wall a moment, and his voice was passive. "I was very hungry one afternoon and stopped at a cabin. Sitting leaning against the side of the door was a girl. About my age. She had her knees up and her thighs showing. I had never seen a nigger of such degradation as that girl. As I rode up, she said, 'Hello, stranger, any 'backy?' I said, no, I didn't have any. She spit and said, 'Who wants a stranger, with no 'backy.'

"I was hungry, though, and went into the house. Dirt floor with trash all over, and some of the trash was more children.

"I was cold and hadn't eaten the whole day. I saw a keg of whiskey on a stand in the corner. I asked the woman if I could have a glass. She began to whine and said, 'I ain't got no whiskey.'

"I said, 'Ma'am, if I'm not mistaken, that looks like a cask of whiskey over there.'

"She stood in front of it with her arms spread apart as if

169

she was fighting for her virtue. 'Mister,' she said, 'I'm a widow with seven chillen, and we got the whole winter to go, and we all got to drink, and by spring there won't be a ration of drink to go around for usins.' Some of the children were so small they could hardly walk."

Madi did not think he was truly conscious of her presence except as a willing receiver for something that had happened to him. She was willing. She was absorbing his old hurt and it came stinging and new to her.

"I got curious," said Harte Trace, "and stayed around that area for a few days. I went to a spiritual meeting on Sunday." He grinned ruefully. "That preacher was a man of fire. Firewater fire."

He grinned, and the acid of bitterness was all through it.

"I can remember what he said and the way he said it. His sermon wrote itself on my brain and I've never forgotten it. It's the thing I used during the war, when I was afraid my principles were wrong and when I wanted to go back to the feelings and beliefs of my kin. Whenever that happened, I thought of the sermon and let it go through my head."

Madi was looking deeply into Harte Trace's eyes and saw no change in them. He suddenly picked up an inkwell and threw it and Madi thought he had gone mad and thrown it at her. The thunder of a shot burst past her ear. She had twisted to one side but had not fallen on the floor. She turned and saw Jenkins holding Sarah Bruce.

The fiery eyes of Sarah Bruce were not turned on the colonel, they were turned on her, Madi.

"Jenkins," said Colonel Trace, "will you escort Mrs. Trace to her quarters?"

The door closed. Harte Trace was watching her. Madi brushed back the edges of her hair. She felt sweat on her fingers.

"Why does she hate me?" she asked.

"Your man won," said Harte. "You wouldn't expect a woman to appreciate it, would you?"

"But to shoot me?"

"Is that so surprising?" he asked. "Let me continue. I'm not only going to tell you what I heard this preacher say, I'm going to imitate him. And you'd be surprised how often in my mind I've had to do this."

He pushed back his chair and got up and began to stamp around and snort.

"My text is from the apostle David. David was an apostle. Try the spirits! David said the stomach is best preserved with a little wine, and what is wine, it's spirits! The ancients called alcohol spirits because they knew, they knew, the gods had handed it down. But get that! The gods! That's idolatry. That's not religion!

"But we got Jesus Christ. And him crucified. That's religion! That's religion!"

Madi watched Harte Trace with fascination. He was transported. He was living the scene that had changed him. He was a backwoods preacher, and his voice hit the ceiling and came back and she knew he was passionate, too. He was acting, but he was in it so deeply it was almost true. As anything can be true that hurts so much with power.

"And what did he do on his last night?" cried Harte. "What was at the last supper. Wine. They drank wine. That's what they drank.

"It's all through Scripture, there's no doubt about it, it's all through there, drink, drink. But I've seen women around here smokin'. Smokin'? I challenge, I challenge. Anybody who can rise up and tell me that anybody in Scripture said a woman can smoke, rise up and tell me. Rise up!

"You can't. You can't do it. You're fixed to your seats, because it isn't Scripture.

"But drink it. Yes, drink is. What was the prize Noah got? You tell me about the prize Noah got. Do you know it, or do I know it, or does God know it? God knows it, and I know it? Do you know what happened on that mountain, Ararat. Ararat, I know that mountain well. I've seen it in my mind. Remember Arat. That's where Noah landed. What happened there? What happened? Noah was the most decent man in history, so the Lord preserved him so Noah could preserve the world.

"Noah got drunk up there on Arat. Yes, sir. He got drunk. Ham got drunk. They all got drunk. God had the vines up there for them and already made 'em fermented, by God, he did, he had a spree ready, by God he did, he was ready for 'em!

"But what whiskey do you drink? I'm reachin' out for you, I want to know what whiskey you drink.

"That's what I want to know.

"Whiskey's in Scripture, but you don't think do you, that the good Lord wants people to give out this whiskey that he wouldn't have wanted on the Ark?

"Can anybody defy me about that?

"Where do you buy your whiskey? That's what I want to know this Sunday. Where do you buy your whiskey?

"You see Mr. Henderson over there, in his pew, sitting with his family. Do you buy your whiskey from Mr. Henderson? Do you? Or do you defy the Lord?

"Do you buy the whiskey from Mr. Tharcher? Do you? You consign your coins to the devil?"

Harte Trace had been shaking, rattling, and rolling around, his hair and eyes and flinging arms. He stopped, took some deep breaths, and sat behind his desk, facing Madi. She had been enchanted. He would have been a good transfixing preacher. She had been subjected to a few of them in the jail, but Harte would have outdone any of them.

"That sermon," said Harte Trace, "is what made me leave the South for the North."

"Why?"

"I thought the preacher might have been confused by his text or maybe by some whiskey. I went up and spoke to him about it. He told me that he could neither read nor write and that he got his subject matter for his sermons from a plantation and store owner, Mr. Henderson.

"I went over to see Henderson that afternoon. I introduced myself and he was as hospitable as a gentleman can be. I spoke to him about the sermon, and he laughed, and so did his friends on the veranda. 'We keep them happy,' he said. 'As long as they can drink in the sight of the Lord and roast a few niggers no wand then, they ain't going to cause any trouble.' "

Harte Trace was still looking off into space, but his eyes cleared and came back to her, and there was no sadness, no regret, nothing but steady green eyes.

"I knew then," he said, "that niggers might not be animals after all. That you could degrade people, no matter how white or blond the hair, or blue the eye. When I had seen that, I decided I would stay on the side that would free anything that walked on two feet. Anything."

With disdain she said, "If a dog stood on two feet——"

He replied, "Anything that can stand on his two feet and face me isn't a dog, and if anybody insisted on making him one, he would have to make an answer to me."

He was not yet good enough!

What kind of courage, pride, ego, you foolish, insane girl! What do you want, Madi?

Everything!

She had thrown the cloak of meekness, of even its pretension, to the four winds, and let any wind carry it away and let it land anywhere, she didn't care.

She wanted to hit him, she wanted to scratch him. She wanted to do something to him.

"Why did you hide the death of your brother, you coward?" She shook her fist at him. "Your paper says you defeated Morgan, but everybody says you were sent here to a prison command because you couldn't fight. Why would anybody be sent to a prison command if he could fight so well he would defeat Morgan?"

"You have true and pretty teeth," he said, "and false ones clatter. I would not like to have a wife with clattering teeth."

"What does that mean?"

"It means you had better lower your voice or I will be angry."

She settled back in her chair, very happy. She had the best antagonist a woman could have. He cared.

Her pinkie was stronger than his arm.

"I selected this command," he said carefully. "The reason I could do that was because of my record. My wishes were listened to, I came here because of Jeb."

This was crucial. "Why did you come here because of Jeb?"

He looked at her with wide-eyed surprise. "He escaped, didn't he? Don't you think I knew that Jeb would move heaven and earth to escape? Don't you think I know he was a bravo?" His eyes saddened and dropped and the dark shadow came over his face once again. "I made a mistake," he continued. "I made a mistake." His voice trailed off.

Madi's back was tense, and she was leaning forward. If oversight on Harte Trace's part had killed Jeb, she would forgive him. Forgive him? Not that only. She would fight with every weapon she could find if anyone else ever suggested again that it was his fault.

"I brought my weak link with me," he said, "Jenkins." He was looking at his strong hands, fingers knitted and making the knuckles white. "I couldn't drop Jenkins. I won't drop Jenkins." He lifted his eyes and they did not flinch. "I won't drop Sarah Bruce, I can't. Even though Jenkins, against orders, left the door of the mill unlocked when the mill was unattended, I am going to keep him with me. This despite the fact that he killed Jeb. That mill was the only weak link in this whole institution—except for Jenkins."

"Why must you keep him?" she asked softly.

His hands unfolded themselves, and as he laid them flat

173

on the desk she saw a slight tremor in them that was gone as soon as his palms were pressing the desk.

"I refuse to accept the brutalization of anyone," he said. "I turned against the South because the slaveophiles had tricked me. They made me think Negroes were brutes, and I believed it until I saw that people, white trash, who looked like me could be more brutish.

"I fought war, and I have killed, but I could not bear war making a brute of a man. It is better to kill him than to make him a brute like Jenkins. War took his voice and did something to his thinking devices. Then he belonged to me forever.

"Elvira and Howard belong to me. Brutalized by acquisitiveness, by this environment, which has always been theirs. I'm not going to desert them. The children have been brutalized by this wild, foolish search that Sarah Bruce has made. I will do my best for them.

"Sarah Bruce was brutalized by a false dream. A dream built on brute power and deception. She killed her brother with it. I killed him so that he would be safe, so she would be safe, so the children would be safe. If I hadn't killed him, it would never have ended. He would have risen from his wounds to fight again and again and again.

"I won't desert her.

"You have heard me angry with Jenkins. You heard me rail against him. But that's because I'm not Jesus Christ. I rebel, too, I rebel against the position I'm in—but it's the position I'm in, and I'll live it in the best way that I can!"

His voice had risen, and silence after it made it seem as if it had risen to the ceiling and shattered. But he hadn't shattered. His face was calm again, his eyes unwavering.

Madi felt sick. The thing that made her feel sick was a thing to avoid, like one of the rotunda rats scurrying near your clothes. She spoke swiftly to avoid the rat that wanted to climb inside her clothes and breathe on her belly.

"Why the false mill," she asked. "Why deceive them so long? The long quest, the torment?"

"Halsey's life," he said.

"But she'll hate you forever, Sarah Bruce will hate you forever. She'll never forgive you, and it'll make everything worse."

The rat was at her hem.

Harte Trace shook his head. "It's all over now between Sarah Bruce and me. She can have no hatred. It was settled when Halsey died. You would have to know something about the South and the code of the duel to understand. Women don't carry on vendetta when there is no male who can fight for them. Especially inside a family. Halsey was her only champion. Now I'm the head of the family. She isn't going to poison my tea. Then, what would she do, wash pots?"

Madi decided on the instant that romantic, dreaming southern women were practical.

The rat had his nose under the outer skirt of her mind. She still wanted to avoid him, but she did not have to do so herself; Harte Trace provided the diversion.

"That isn't so in relation to you and Sarah Bruce," said Harte.

"No," Madi said with spirit, "she can always kill me and then you can get someone else." She was about to add that the next one he got could be a pretty young woman who had been brutalized by a cannon and had lost a leg.

The rat was screaming under the skirts of her mind. The rat was her fear that he was taking her, Madi, because she, too, was in her way a cripple, had been brutalized by dungeon, fear, despair, and humiliation. He would not leave her behind either, even as Jenkins?

He was killing her rat for her even before his words penetrated, or were acknowledged by her. His words and their import drifted into her mind after they were spoken. She had been afraid to keep up with them.

"I'm afraid," he said, "that I invite you to the house of the sick. I would be afraid to do so if you hadn't given evidence that deprivation and injury only make your spirit firmer and stronger. I think of you as I think of the people I care most about, those few indomitable spirits that nothing can vanquish. The myth of Sarah, the ghost, who could not be whipped into repudiation of her nature. Jack Morgan, who escaped to fight again. Jeb, who would rather die than be imprisoned here.

"And maybe he was right. Maybe I was wrong in trying to keep him here until the end of the war.

"I invite you to a haunted plantation where your life will be in danger. I am not going to plead my love for you, you must not take that into consideration. You must think only of the fact that you are young and strong, and free now. Free. Do you want to go to prison again? That is what the plantation will be, a prison. This time, however, you will be a warder, but doesn't the prisoner imprison the person who keeps him?

"I invited you to a prison once, it is not my right to do

so again. I'm selfish. I admit it. I don't want to go mad with haunted dreams, an old plantation, Jenkins, Sarah Bruce, three disturbed children, and three Negroes who have been freed but can't permit themselves to admit it.

"I'm selfish. I invite you to danger. I'm a prisoner and sick, too. If I were healthy, I would brush off all this foul air and go to the West and breathe and begin a new life. I can't. I am a prisoner. I was a prisoner of the visions of the South, and I escaped to fight against it but was brought back into it by concern for the fate of my bravo brother in a prison, and now I am ruled by responsibility forever because I killed my brother, through Jenkins, and then killed Halsey, and I am in chains until the end of my life!"

He stood up and crashed his fists on the desk top. "Don't come with me, don't come with me, Jesus, don't come with me!"

She stood up and slapped him smartly across the face. He stood straight and the hysteria stopped in his throat. "I'm not afraid," she said.

They met each other around the corner of the desk and were locked in a rocking, powerful embrace that filled her to the brim.

I am Madi, she knew.